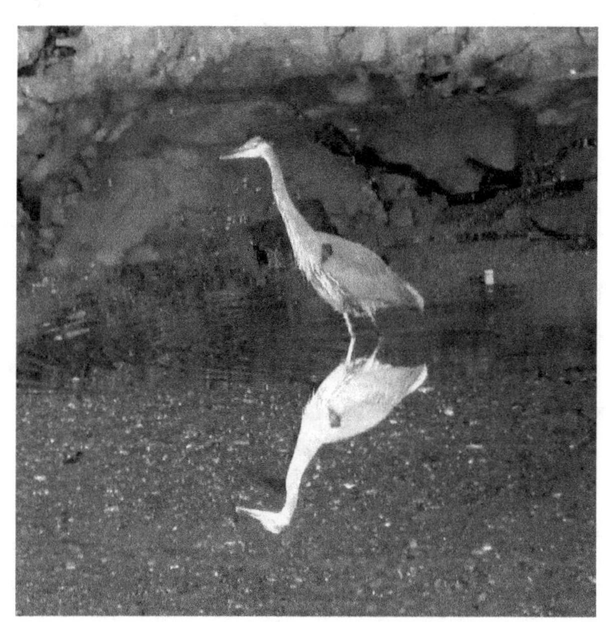

I0836917

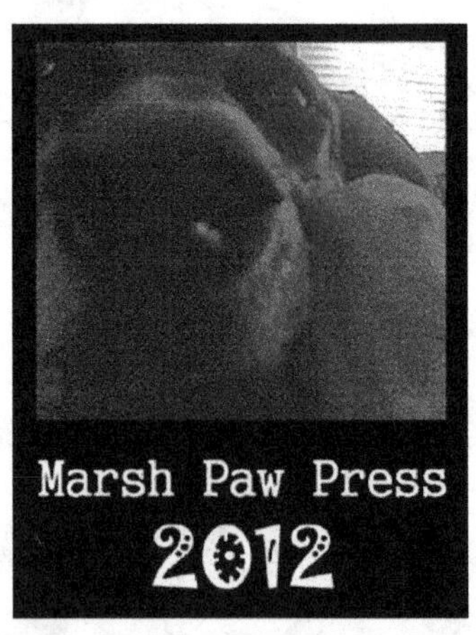


**www.marshpawpress.com**

**www.lulu.com/spotlight/marshpawpress**

# Finding The Secret Sea

An experiment in spontaneity of image/word association

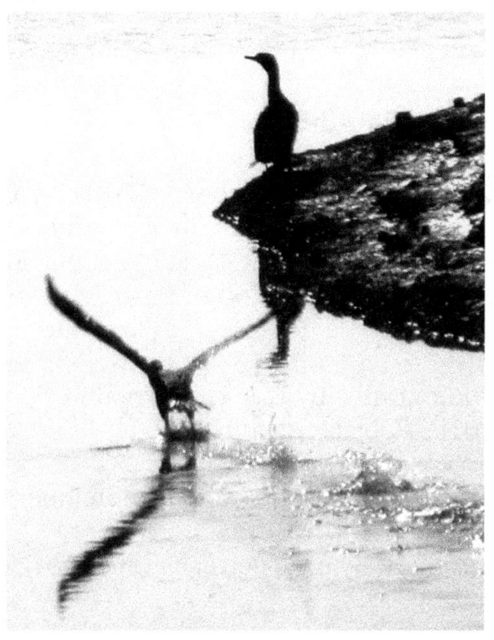

Sketches By Eric C. Harrison

Words by Mike Maguire

**Marsh-Paw Press**

**2012**

# Finding The Secret Sea

**An experiment in spontaneity of image/word association.**

Copyright © 2012 Eric C. Harrison & Mike Maguire.
All Rights Reserved

ISBN 978-0-9888040-3-6

All Rights Reserved Under Standard Copyright Law. No part of this book may be reproduced in any way, shape or form without written consent of Eric C. Harrison or Mike Maguire. Short quotes or the reproduction of a single page may be used for reviews.

Sketches & Photographs by Eric C. Harrison
November, 2011 - February 2012.

Words by Mike Maguire, June 2012 – September 2012.

End Notes presented by S. Spectre, October 2012

Published by:

Marsh-Paw Press
Saltmarsh, Ma.
2012

For information write to - stilldiseased@aol.com

* First Edition Paperback - October, 2012.

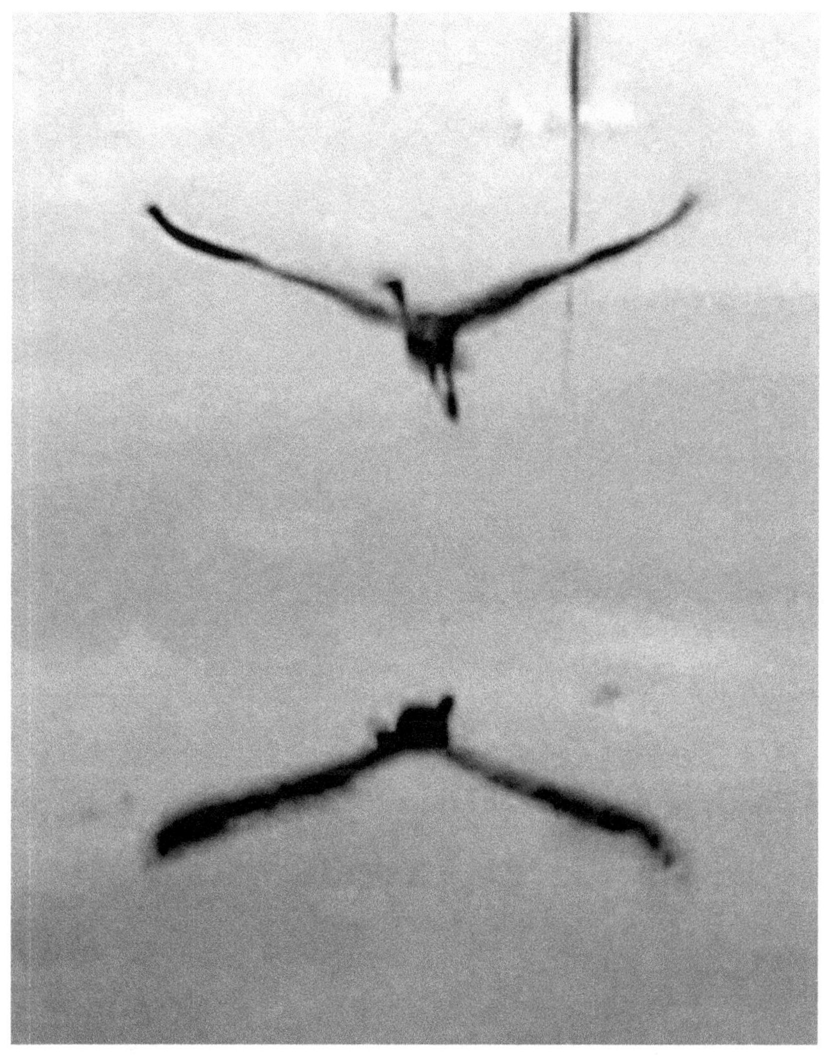

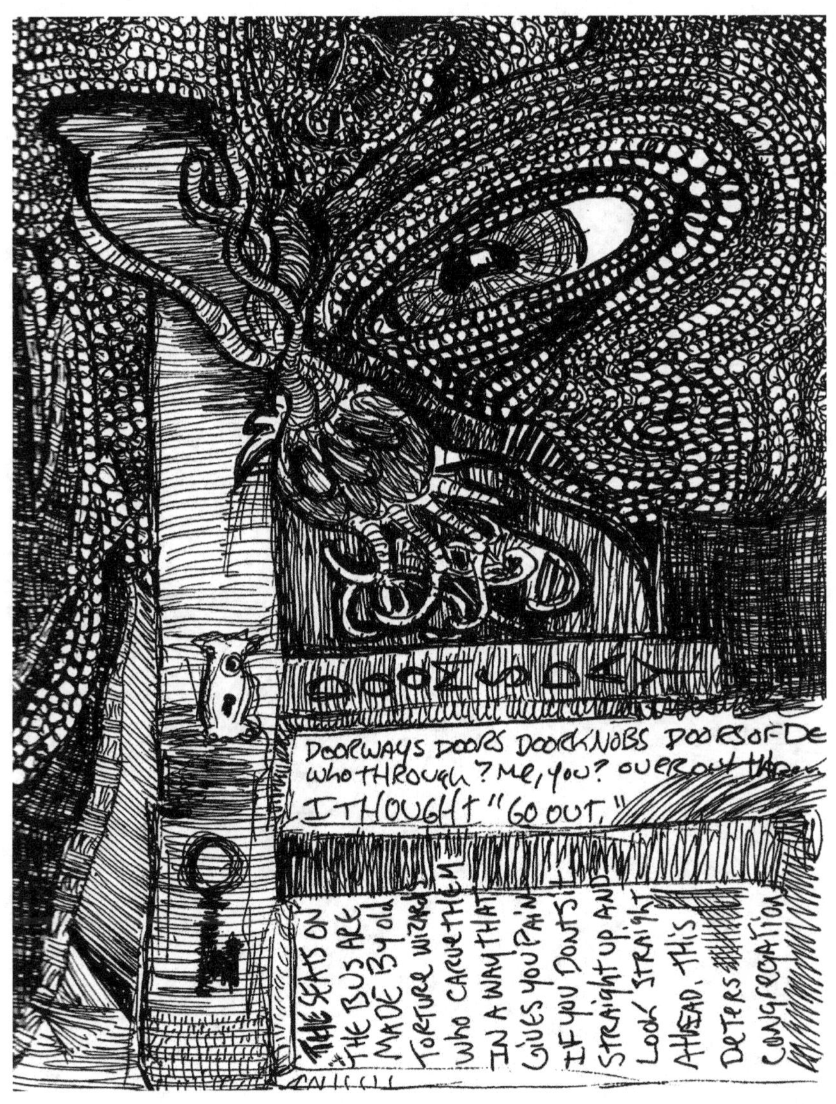


She found the key
on the darkest day
the town had had all winter.

The door was open.

No one was home.

There were notes about storms
and electrical currents
and why light will shepherd only those who walk
with bowed heads.

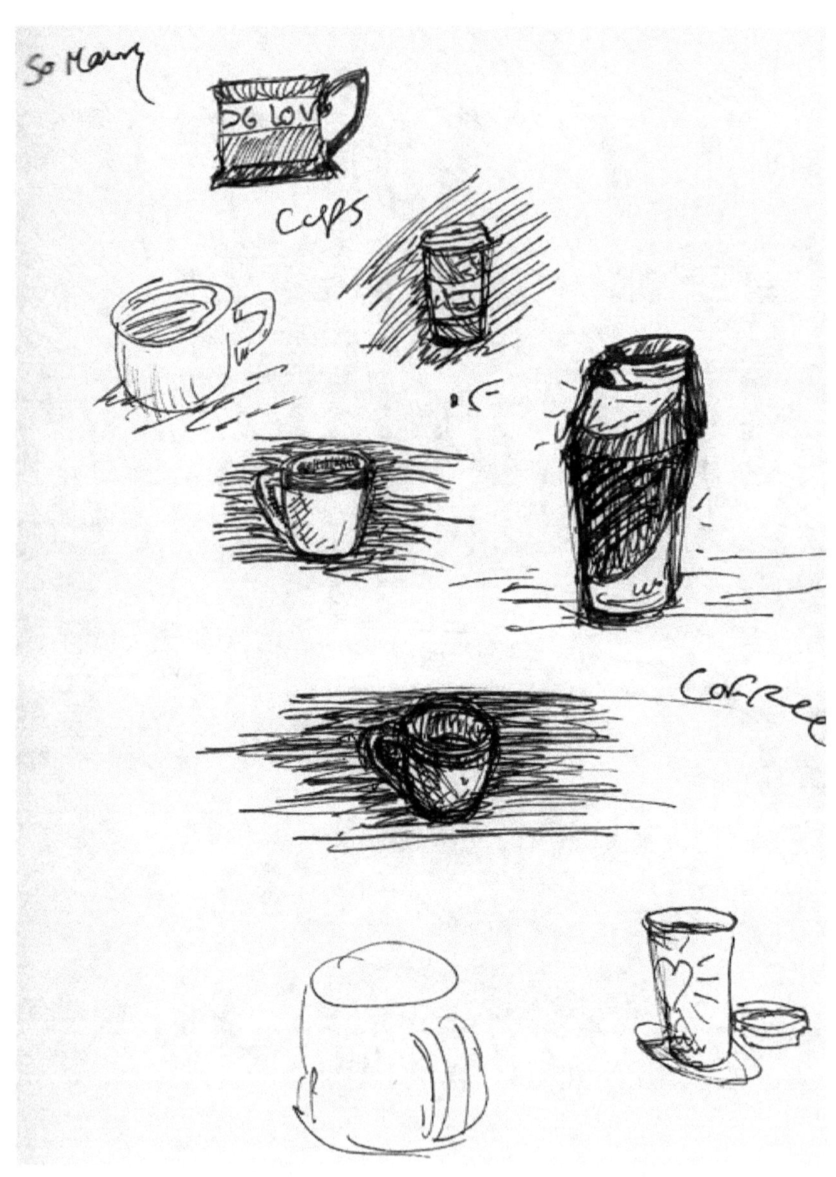


Caffeine was her primary fuel,
usually at the expense of genuine sustenance.

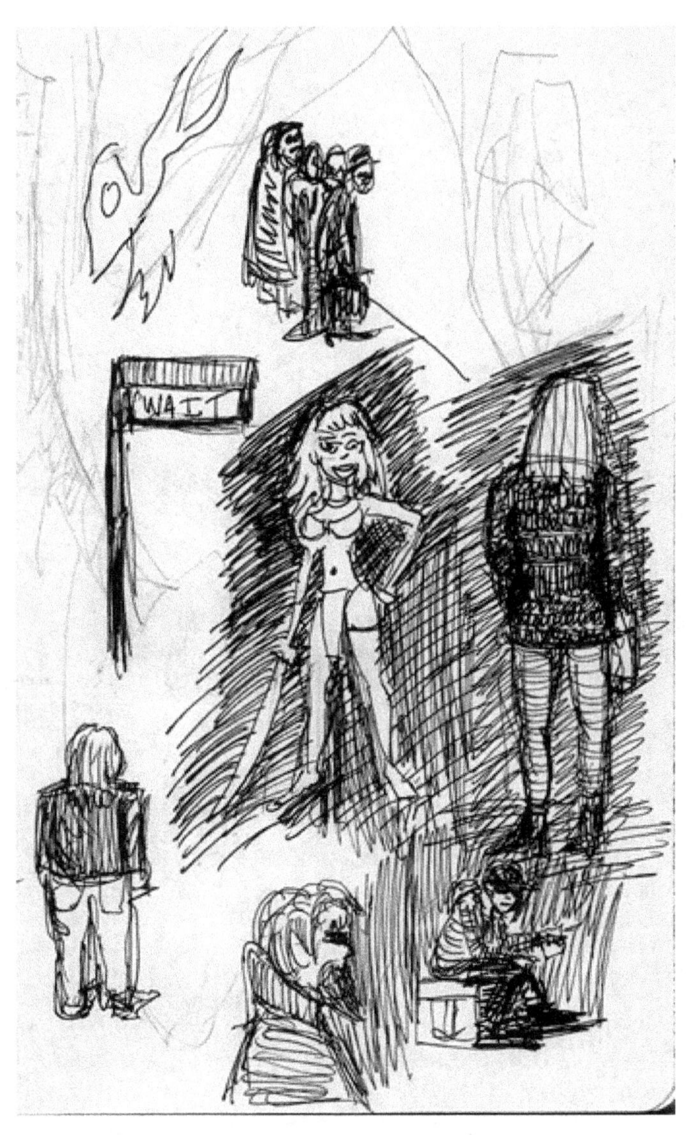


She used to dream of living in the city
until she did.
Now she had nightmares of it.

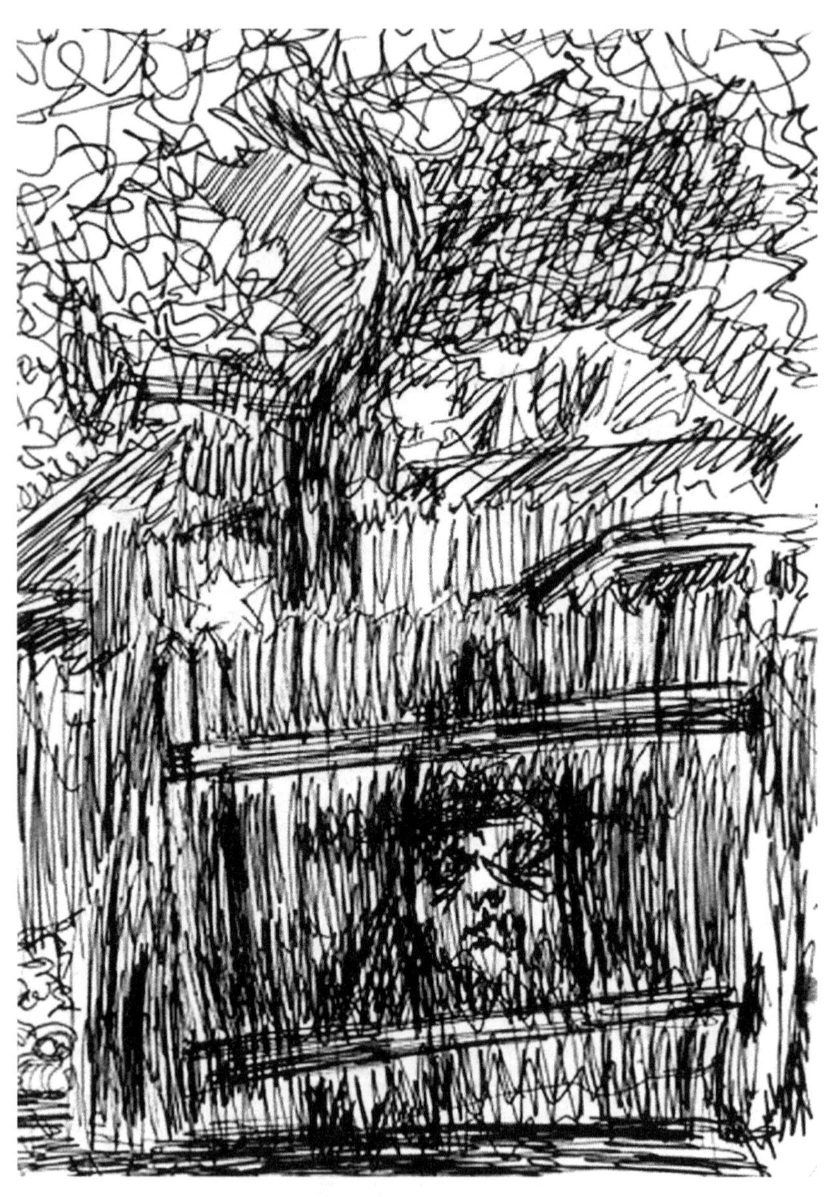

Where was he today?
Again and again she saw his face
but only when imagined.

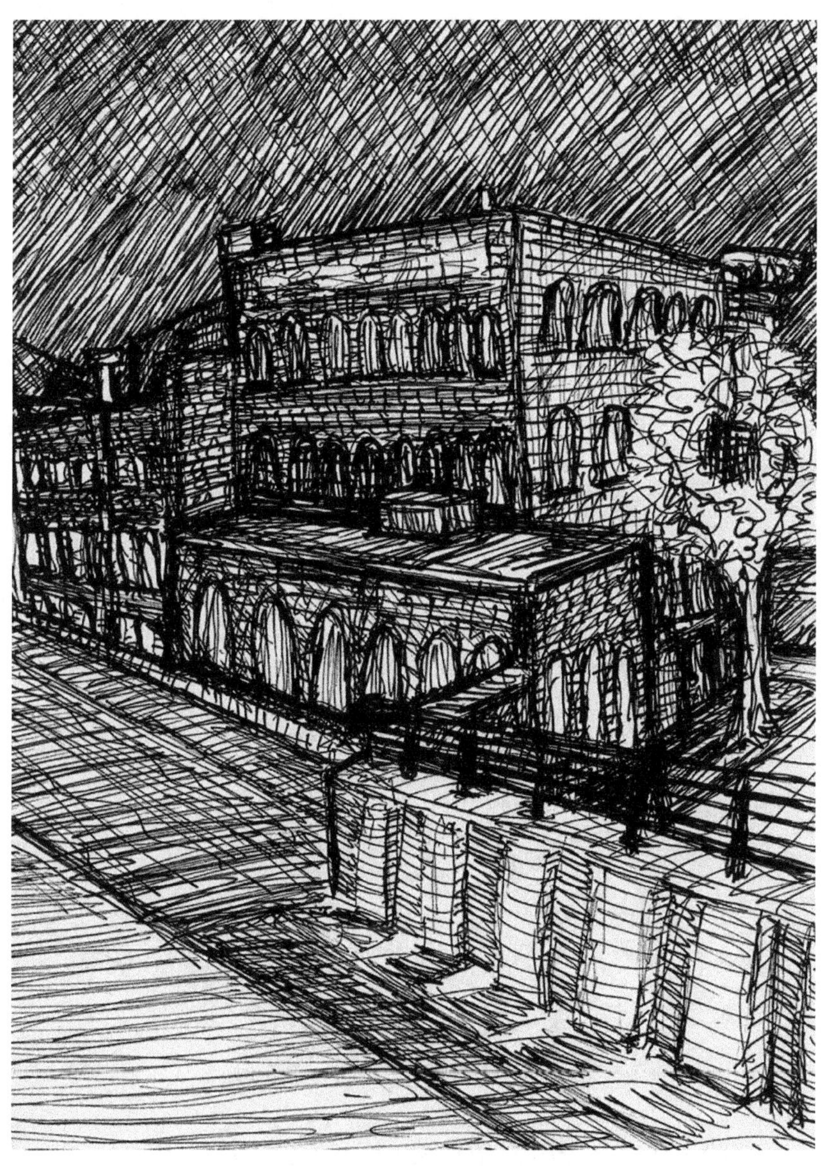

Which was the servant:
The building or the road?
The dock or the canal?

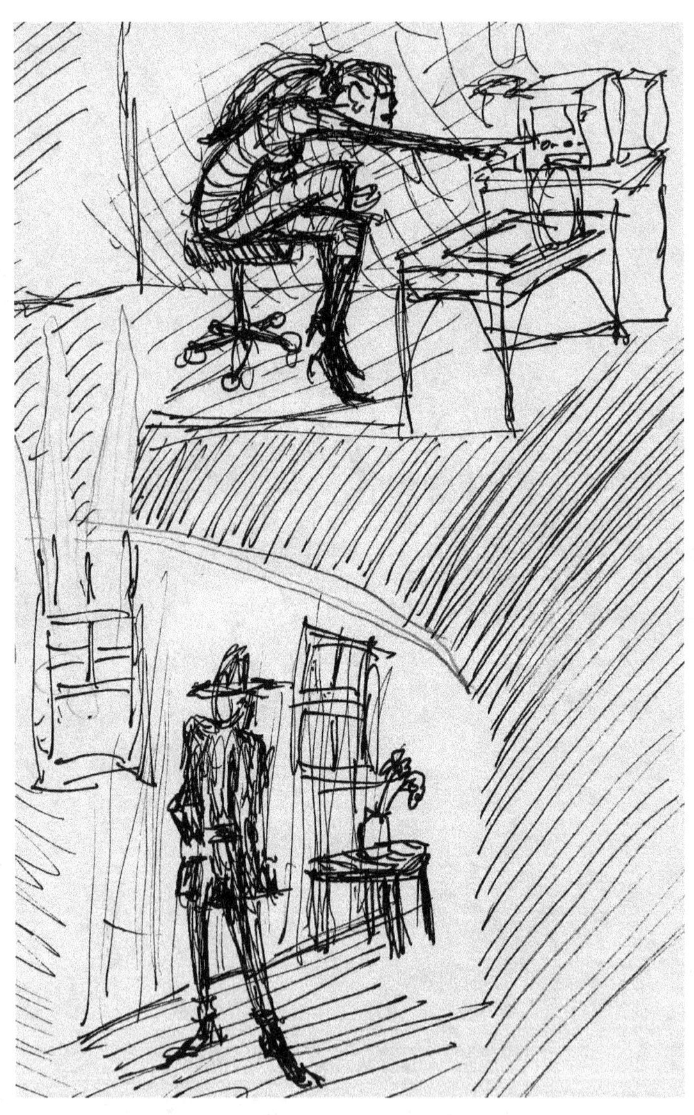

She searched for keys and antiquities
until the screen
and her waking electric dreams of him
became one.

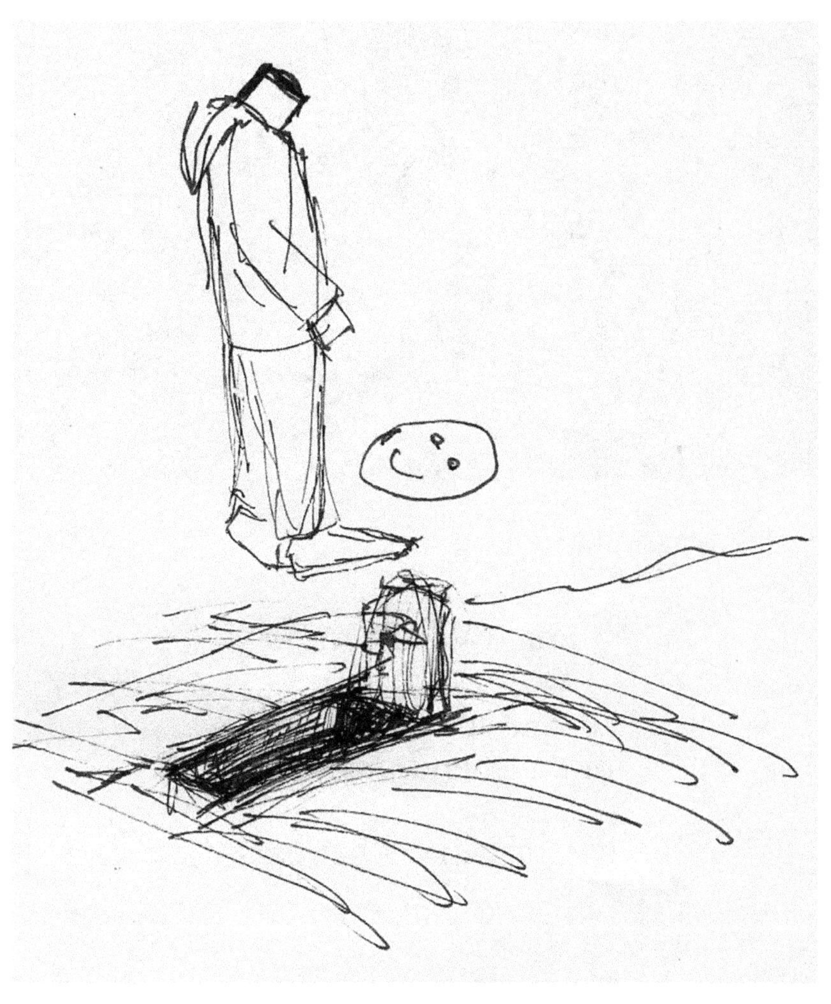

The wind carried nightmares

from across the ocean

and from across time.

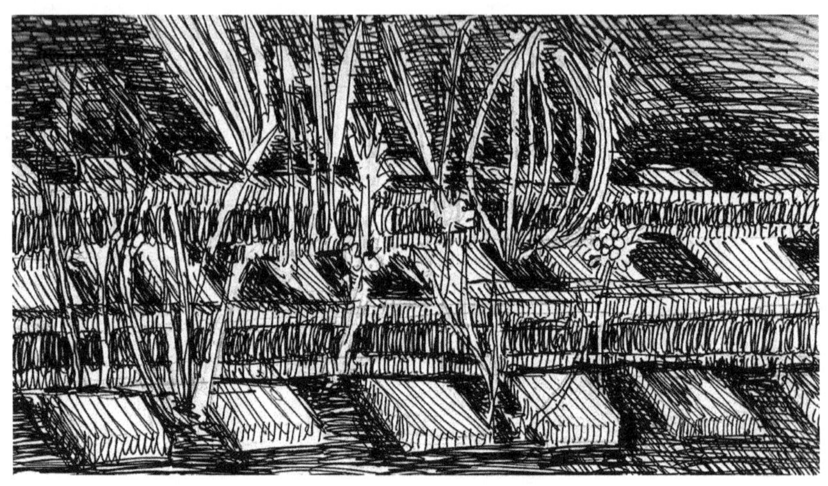

She walked between

the cracked metal
of the abandoned tracks,

briars grabbing at her pant legs.

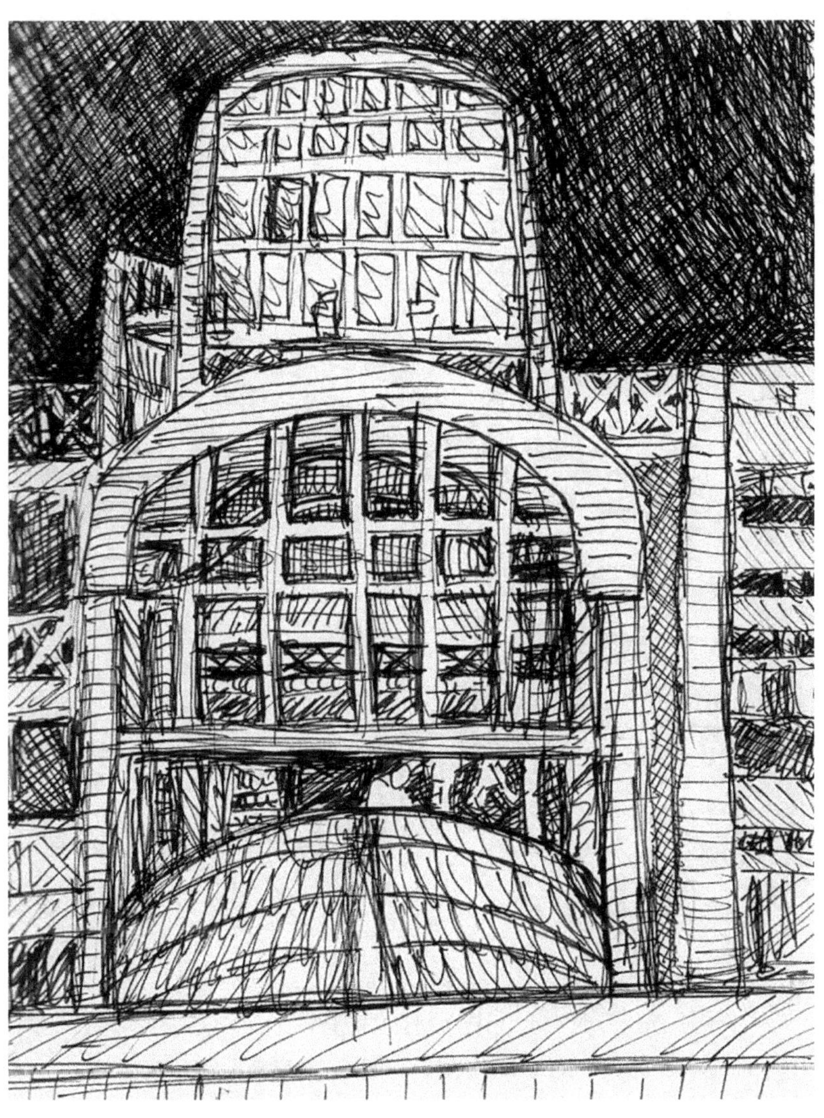

The records in the judiciary center
were the memory of the town,
every marriage, death and arrest
preserved long after relevancy.

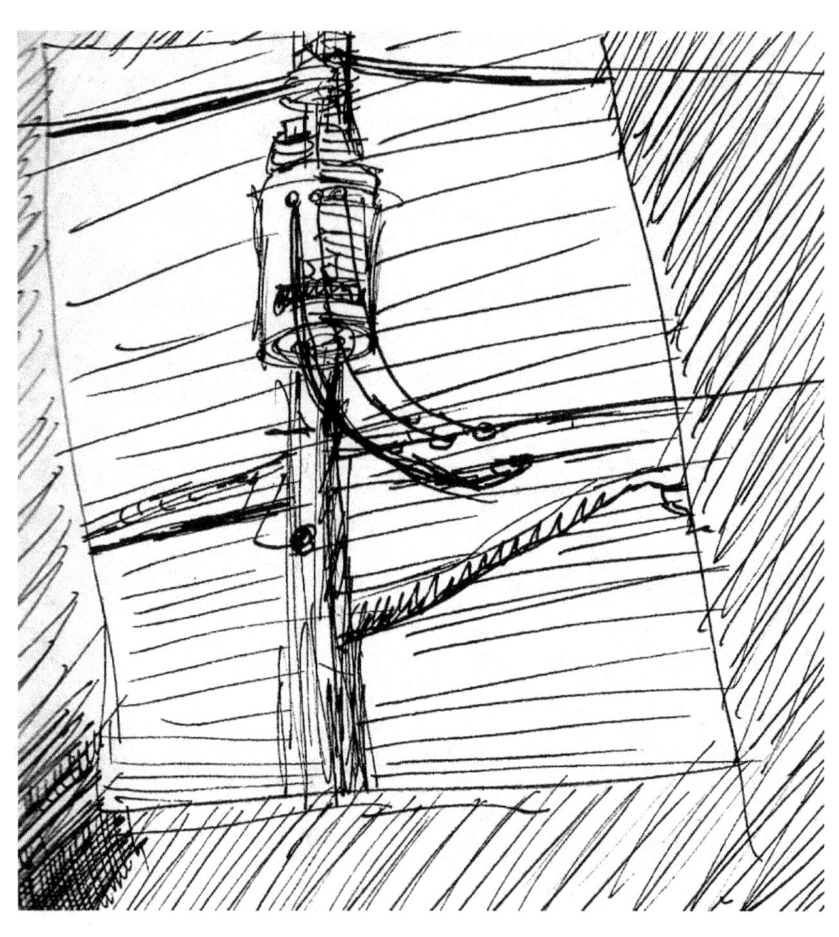

She thought
of how the old infrastructure had been

patched

to the point of being mostly patches.

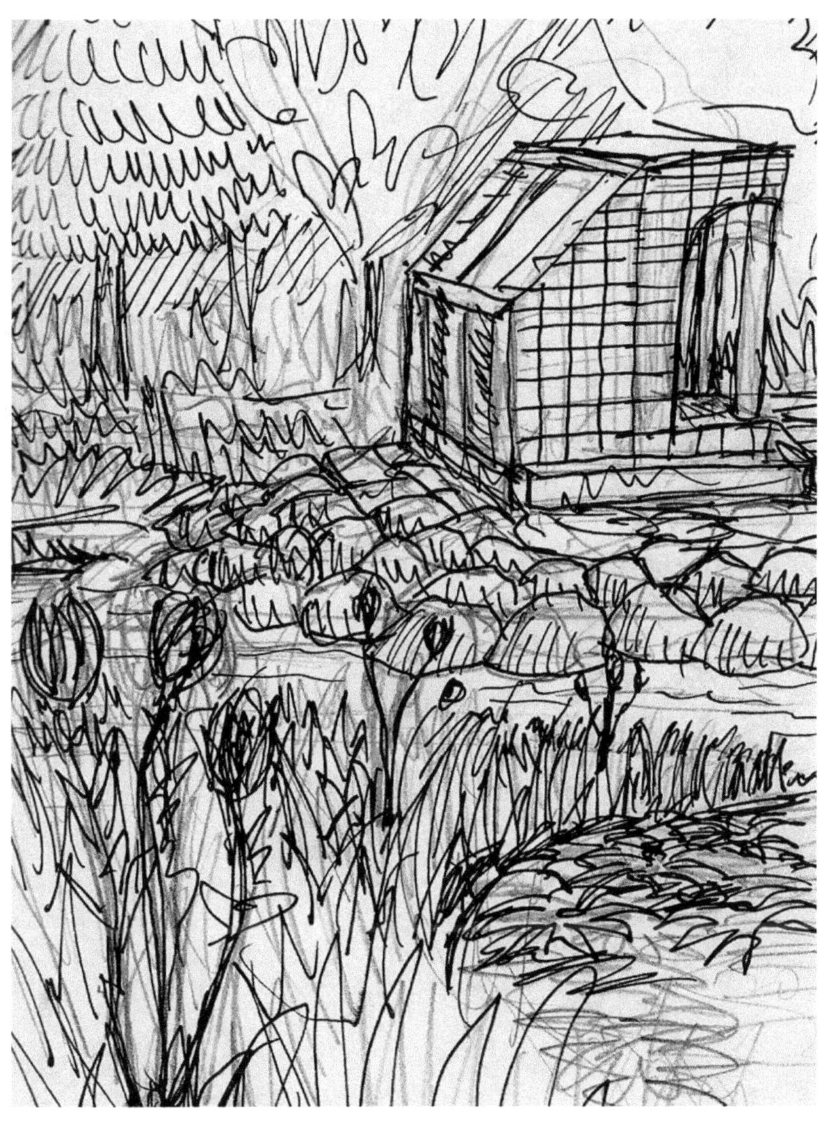

The landscape left people disoriented.

It was ordered but without logic.

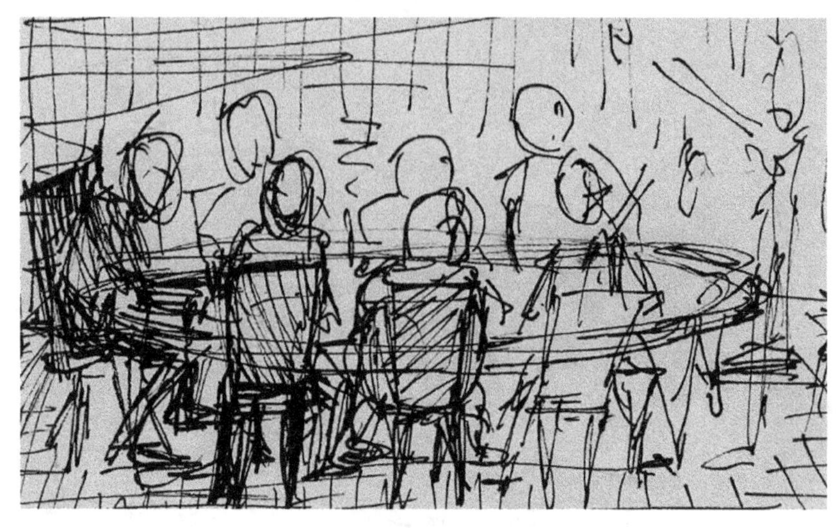

How many tyrannies
are prepared

and passed around tables,

so much meat for the gullet?

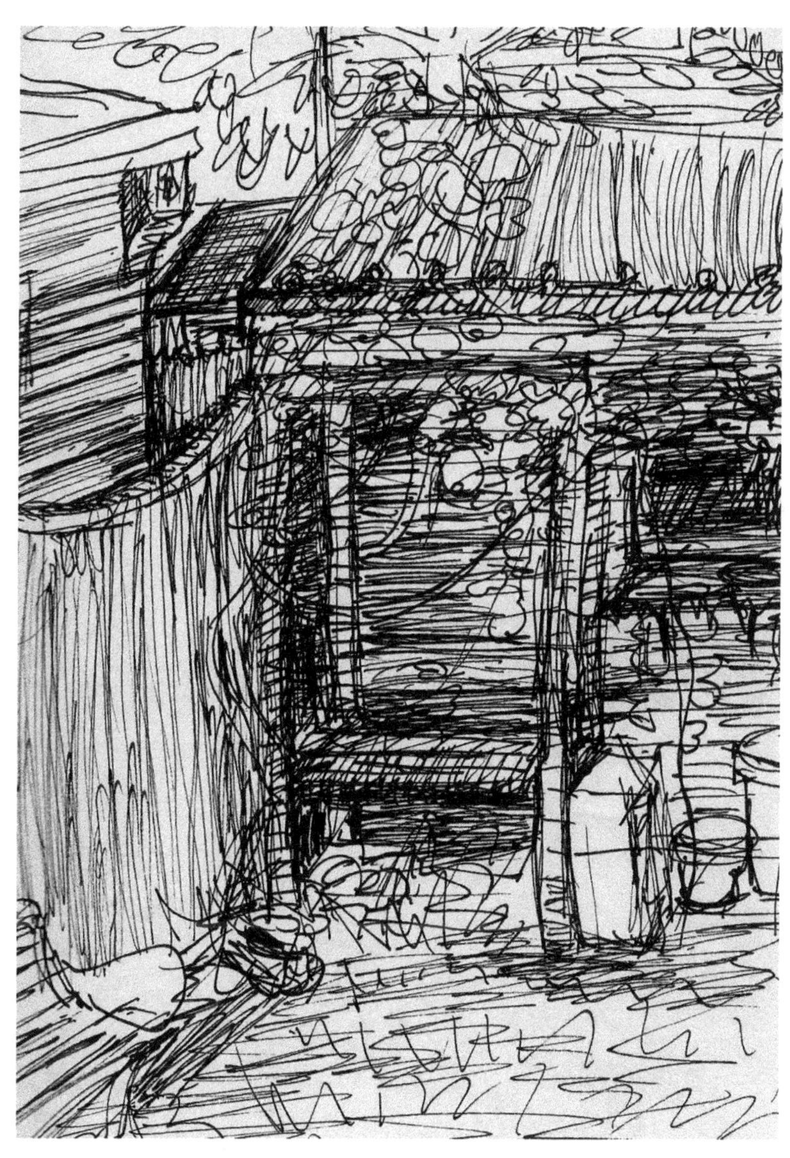

Let nature have the alleys.
Let them become
the courtyards of the free.

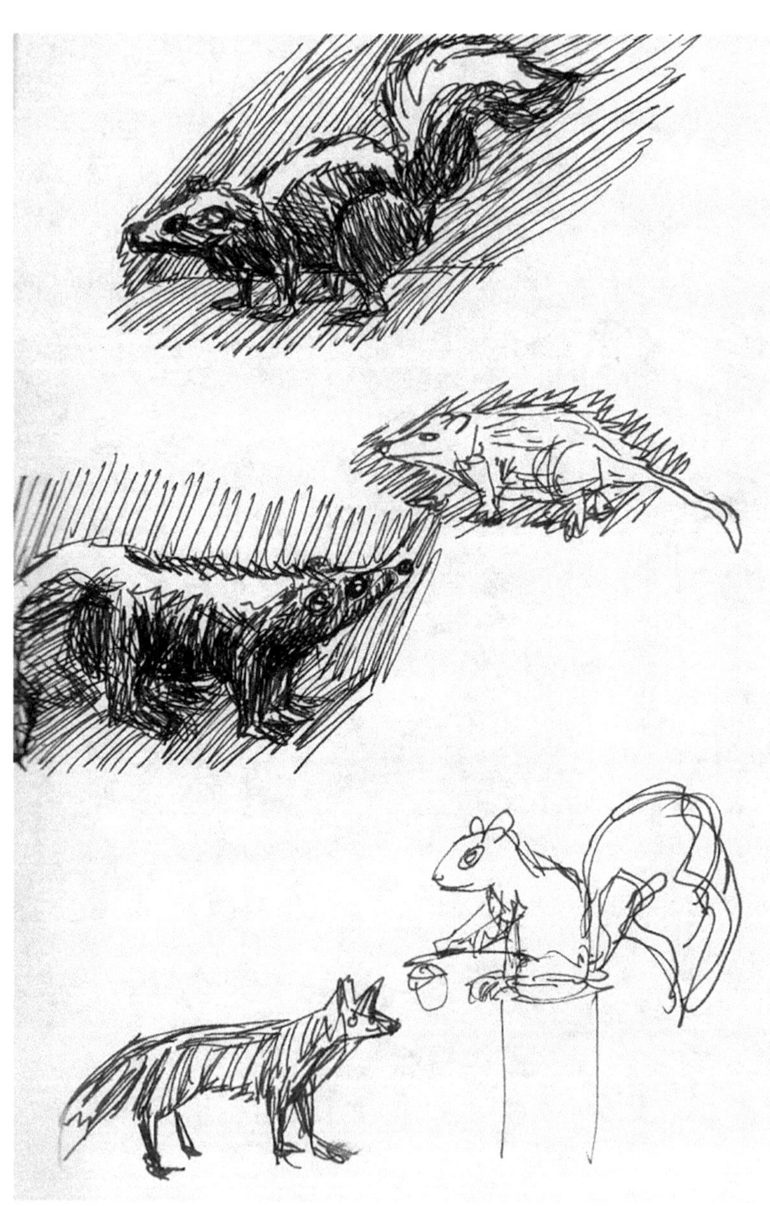

Sometimes we need reminders
that we are all the hunted.

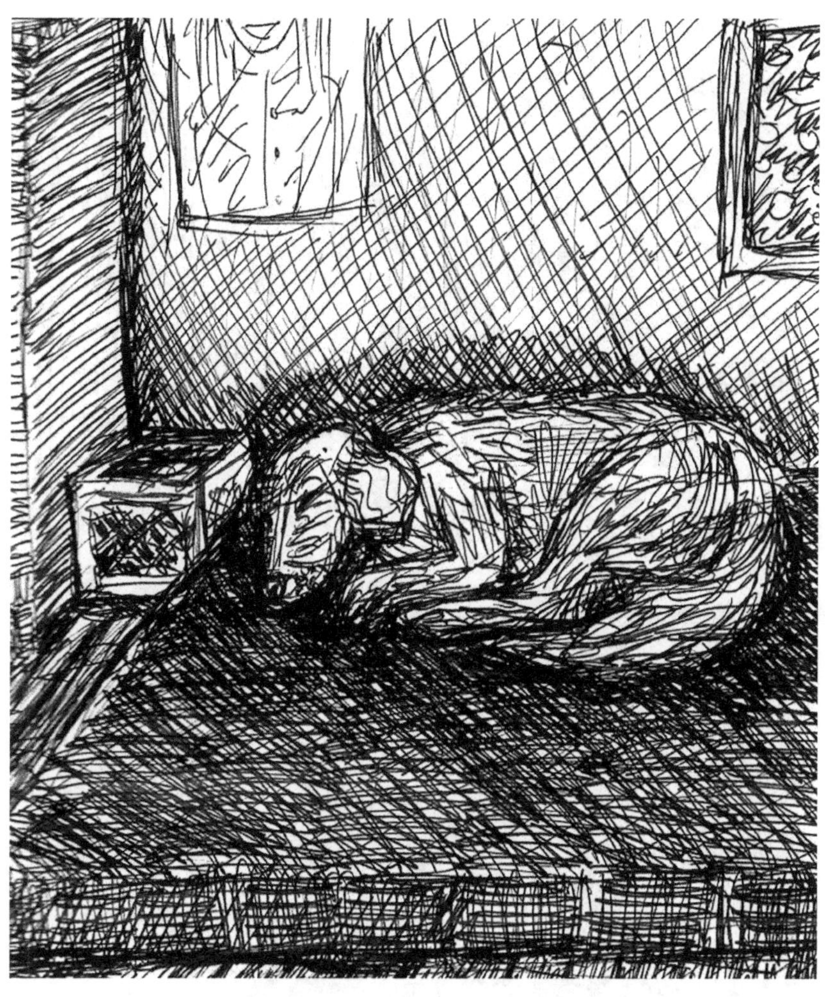

Sometimes we need reminders
that we can only find peace
in the peace of others.

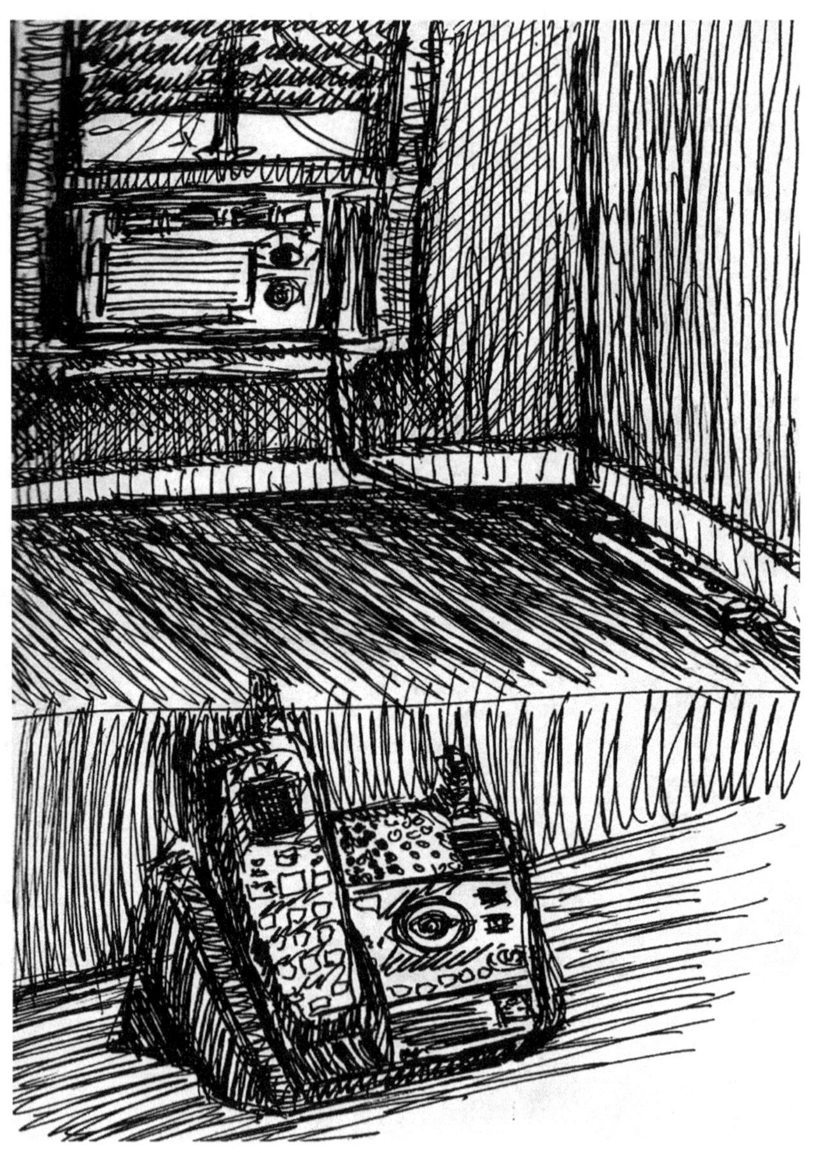

Emptiness is not about space.

Emptiness is about separation.

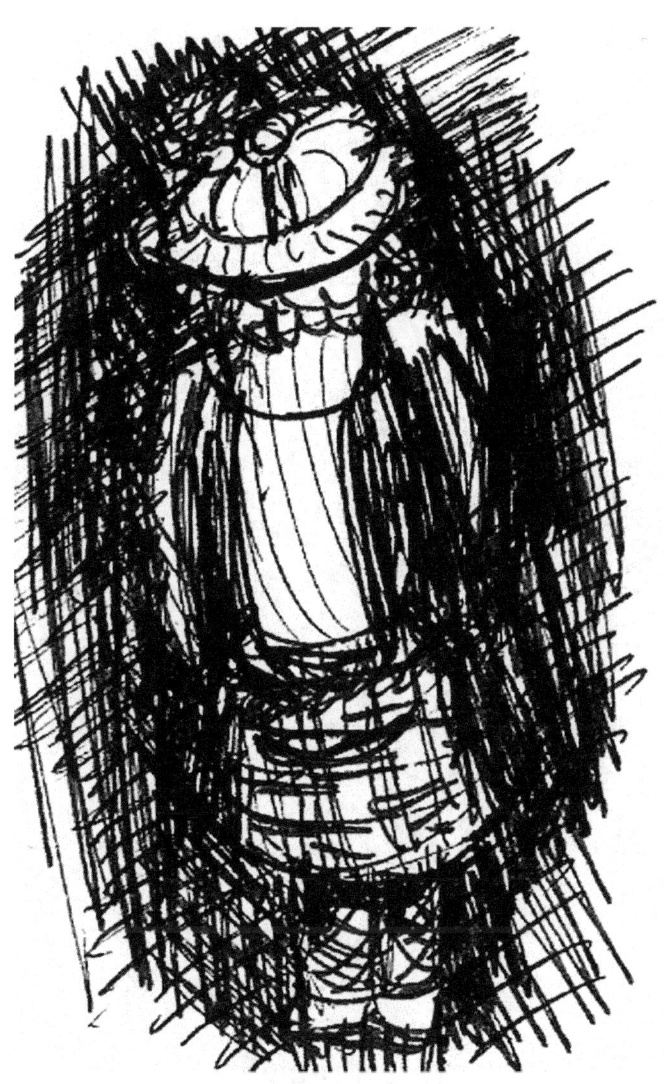

It occurred to her
how she must be
as faded in the memories
of those gone from her life
as they are in hers.

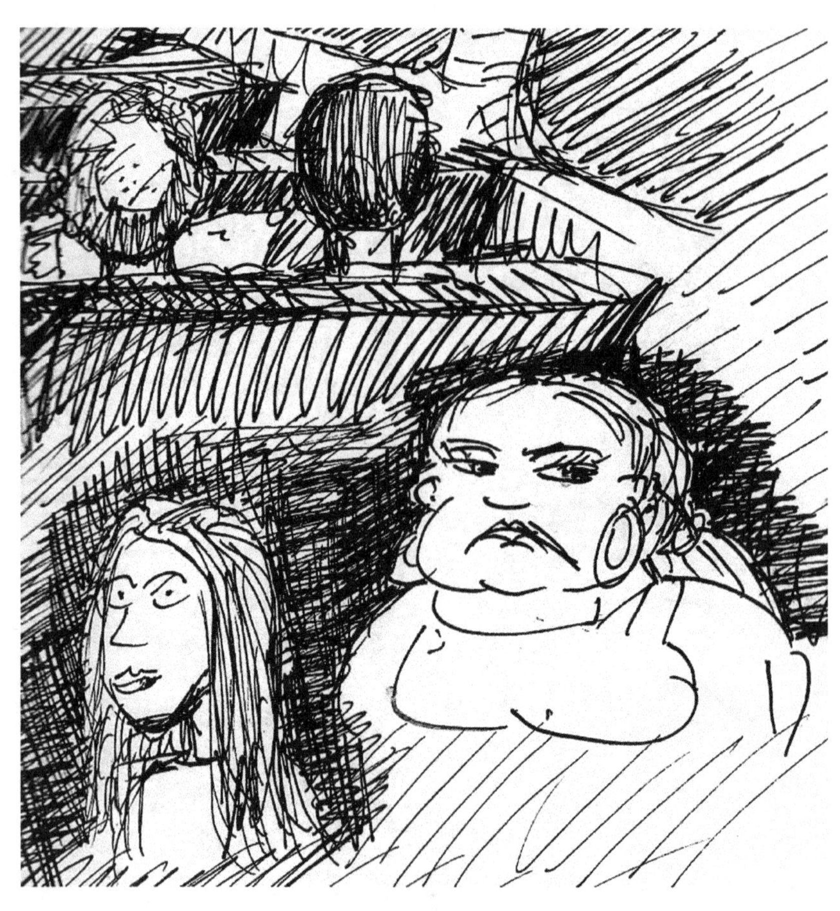

Now
the only ones she could see
with clarity
were strangers.

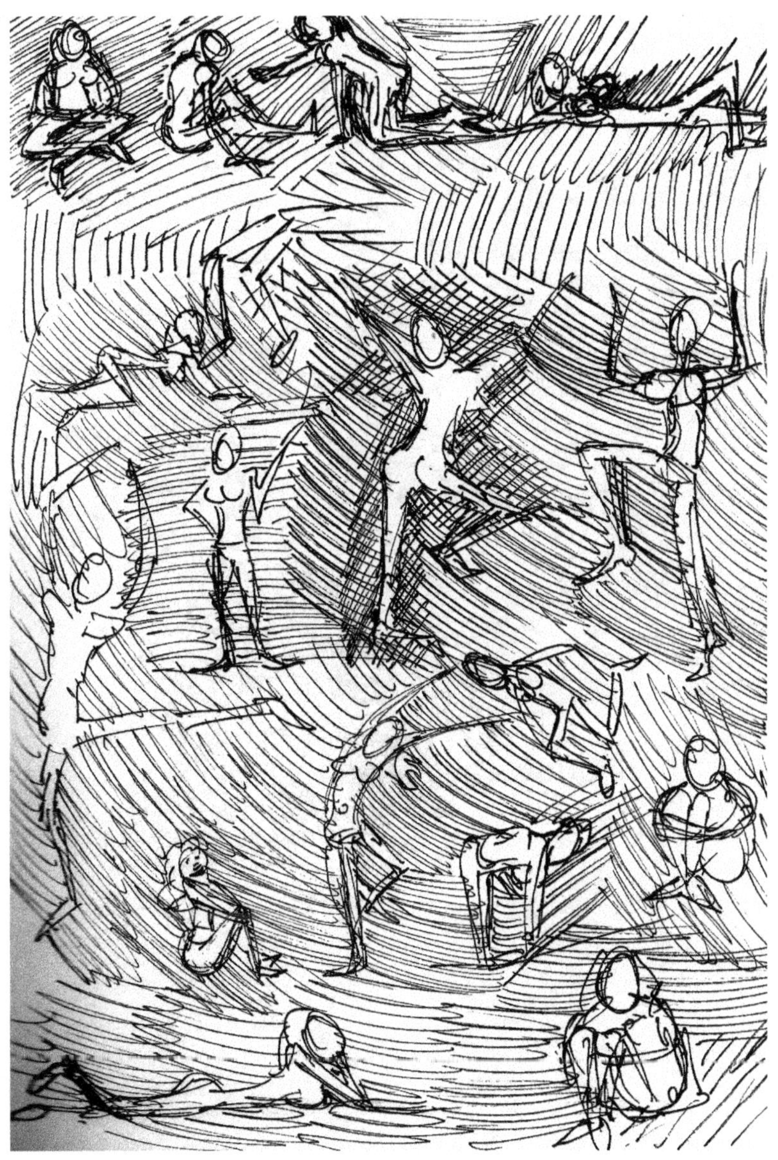

Now it was time to think through
the things that can only be thought through
after their consequences have manifested.

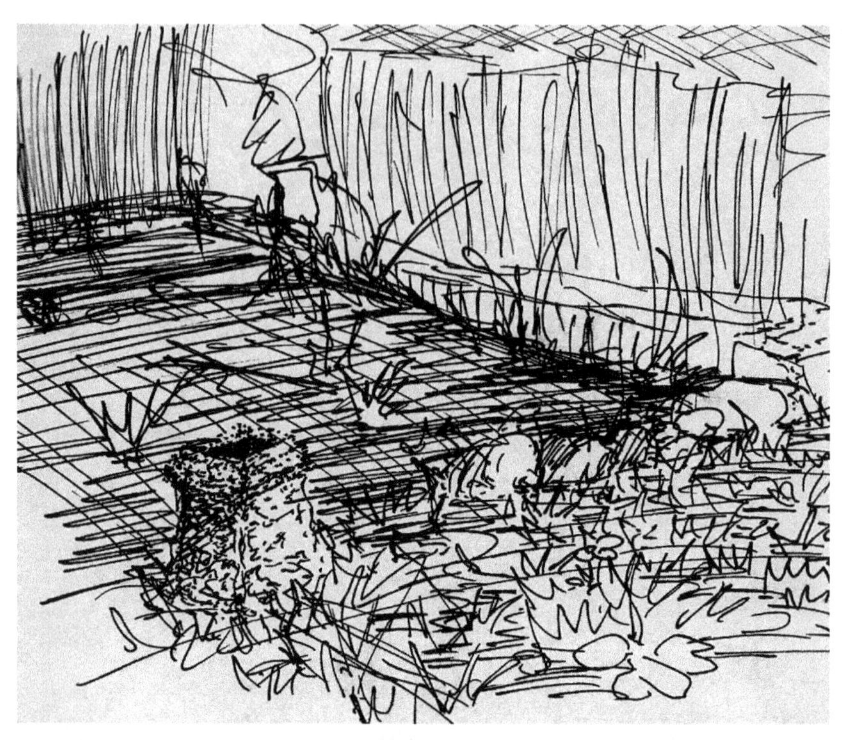

Shadows awakened in corners.

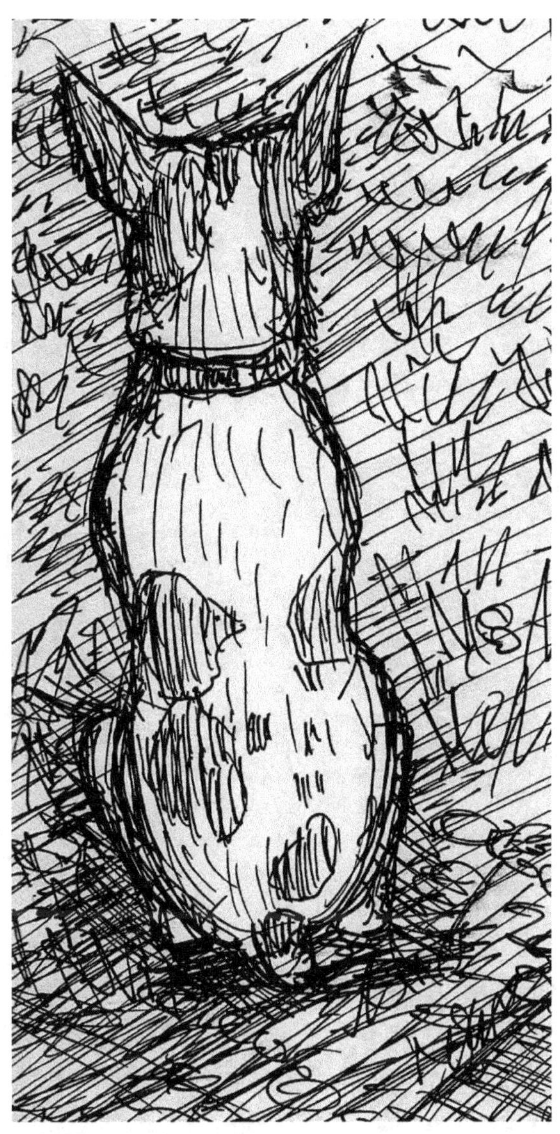

She believed being with a dog
would make her more alert,
would open her world
to secret transmissions in the air and soil.

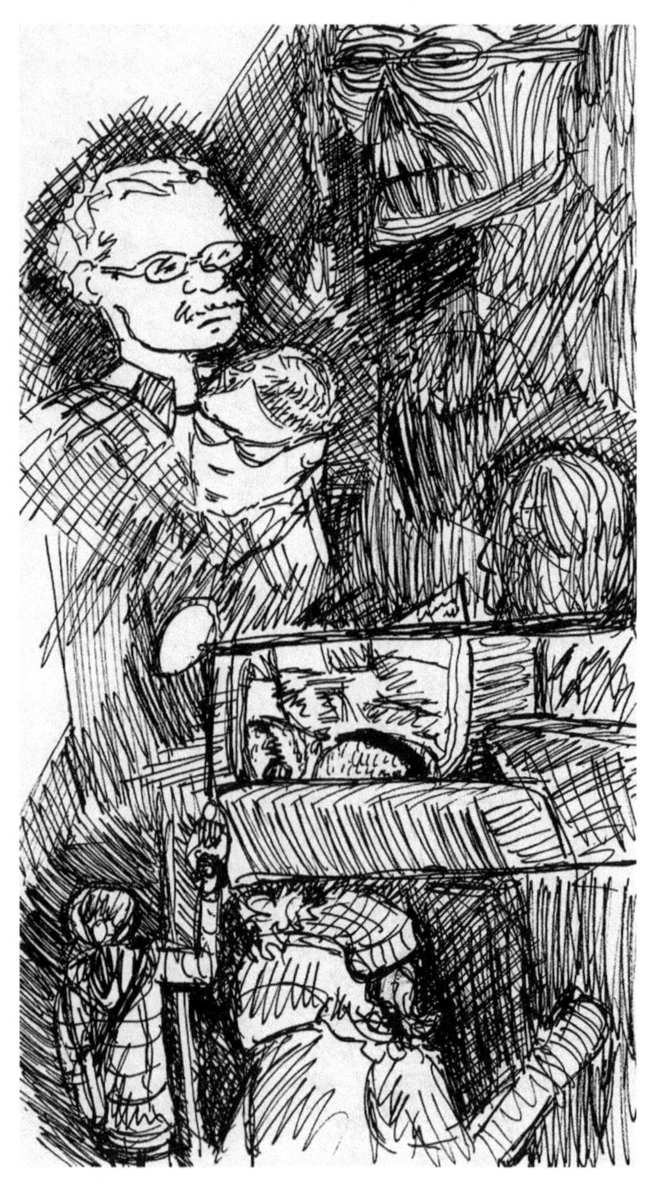

Travels at night stacked up

like people in high-rises.

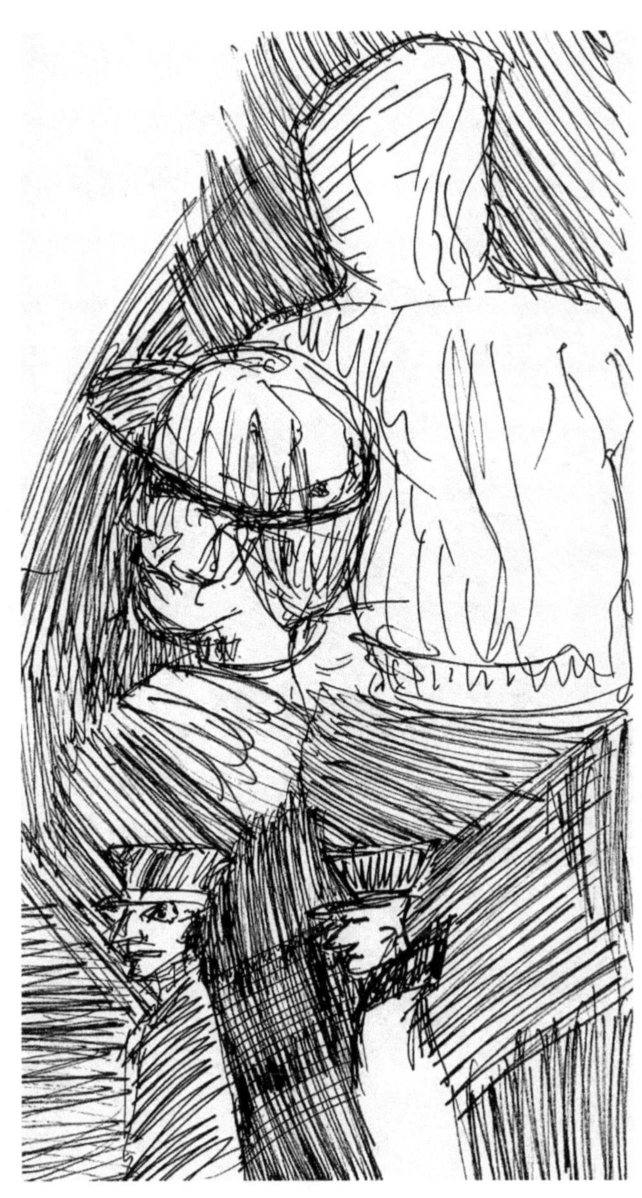

The train station
inhabitants always seemed like
actors sent to film a part.

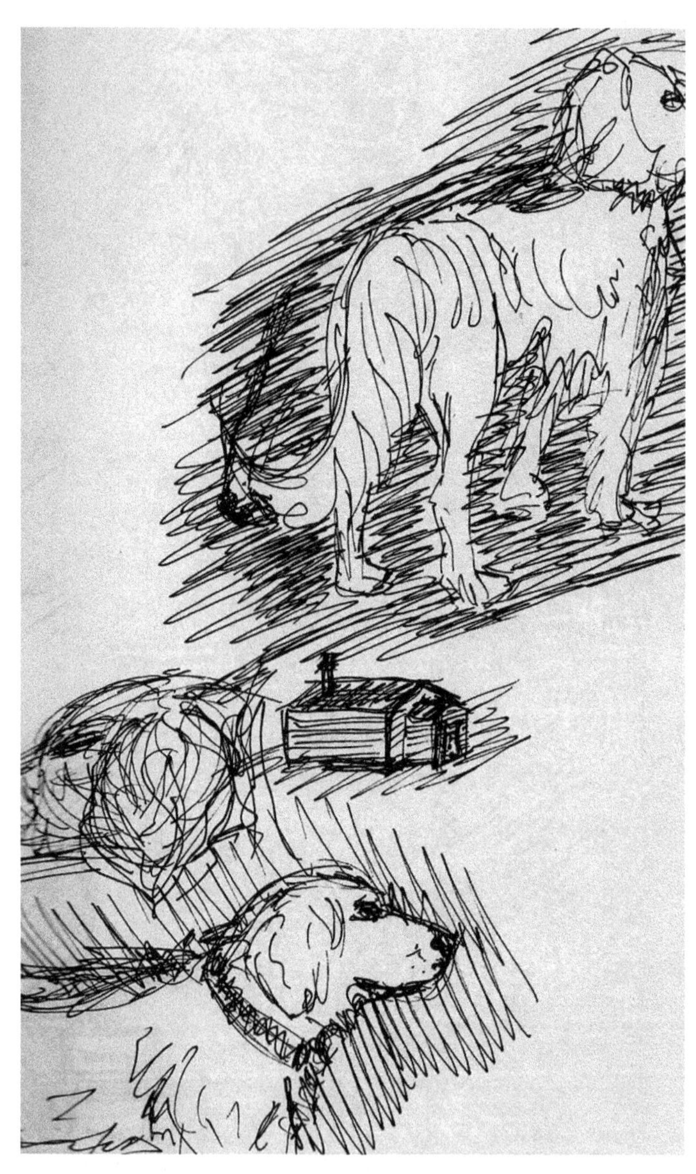

What did the dog see in his mind's eye?
What did he expect
when he turned in a new direction?

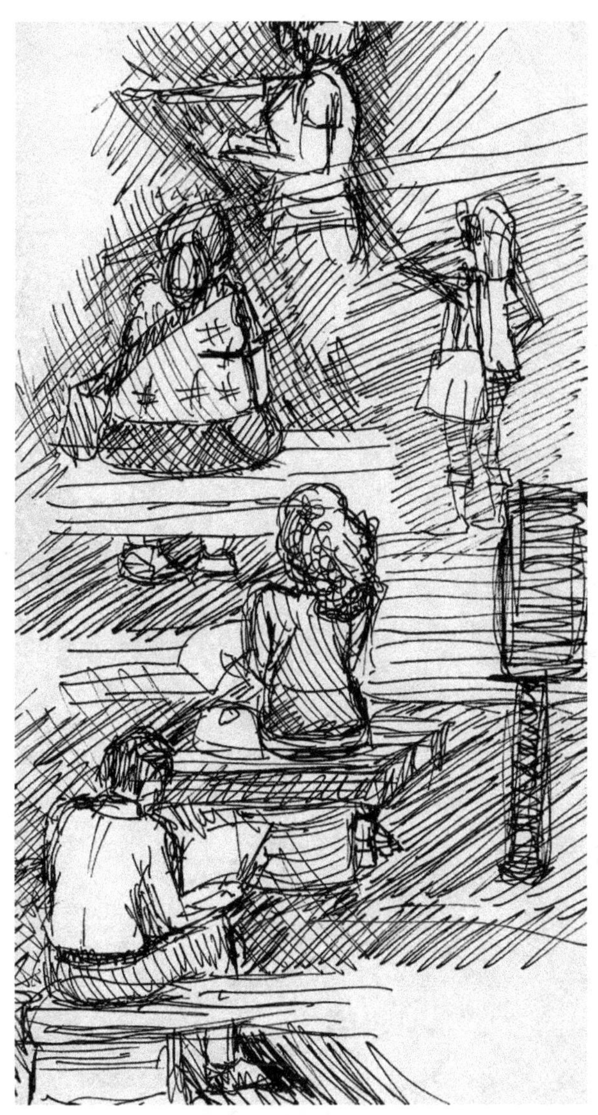

Everyone could be viewed as either
a carrier of lies or a carrier of truths.
Which way she would view them was a choice
between self-preservation and humanity.

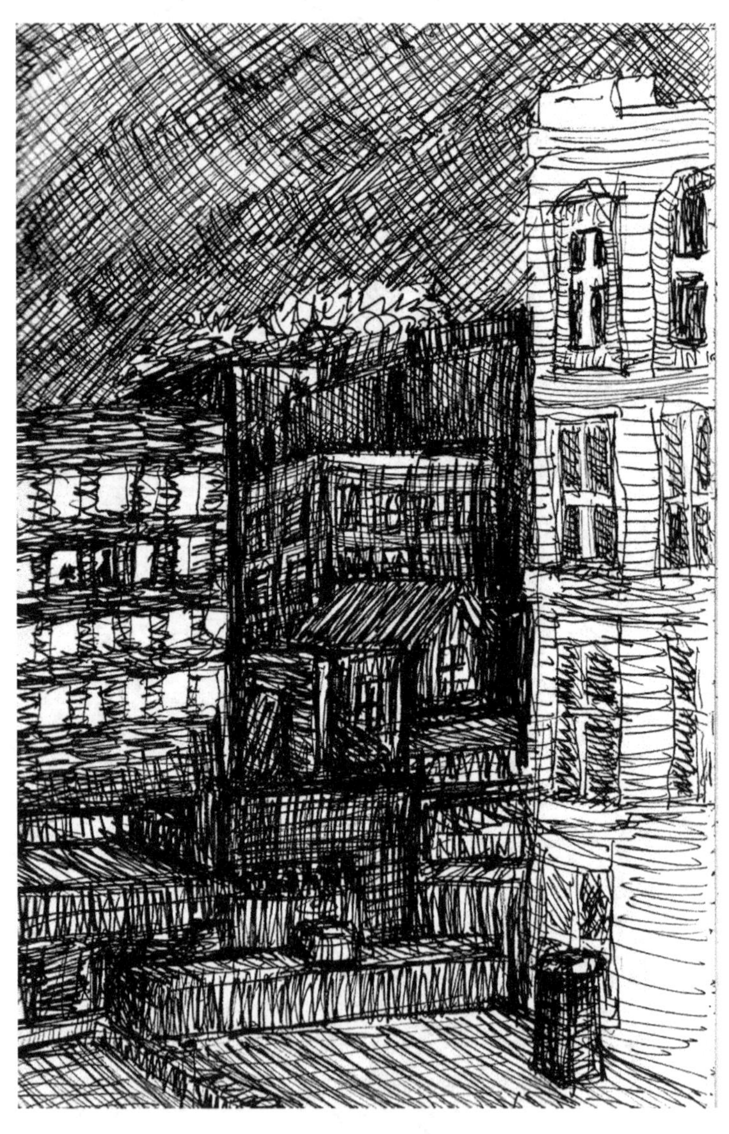

Silhouettes gave the clearest pictures of people.
Without filters
she saw too much at once.

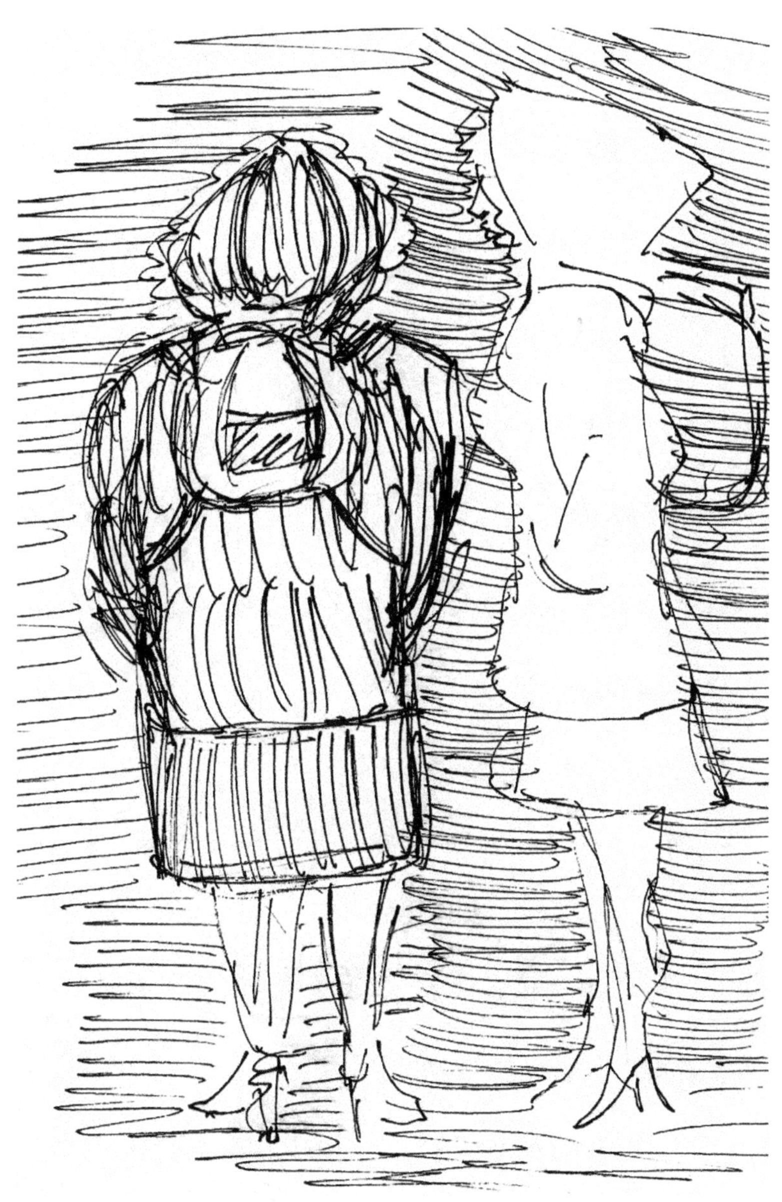

She felt for people who wore jackets
long after warm weather had started.

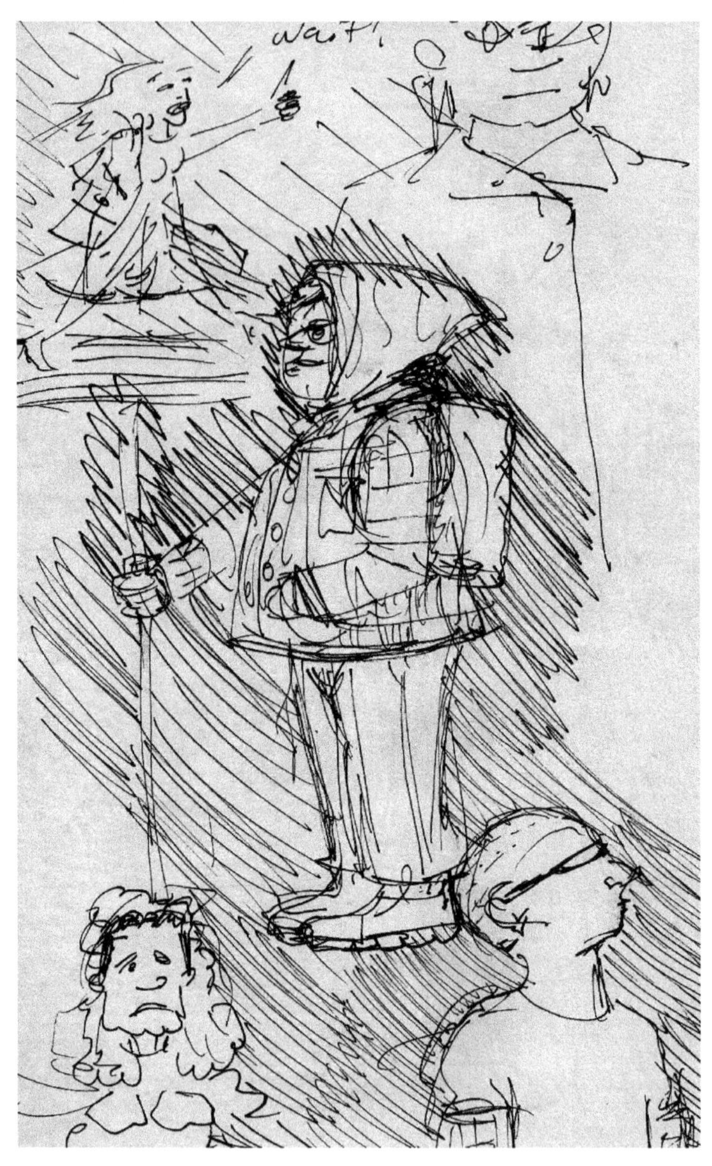


No one was ever happy at the bus stop.
They always thought they had got there too early
or too late.

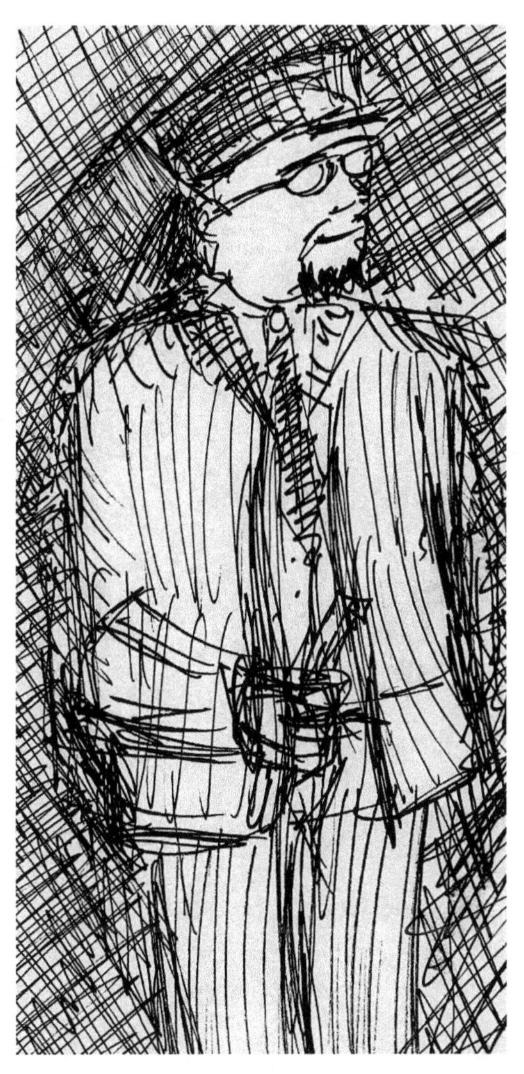

Those optimistic about their destination
will attract both
the good and the bad.

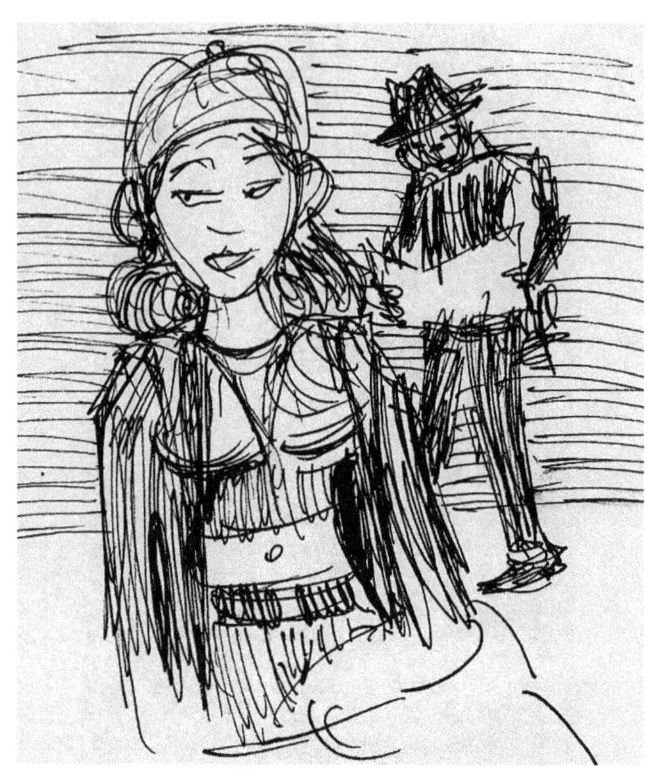

Even though the man looked lost

she suspected his map

was a prop.

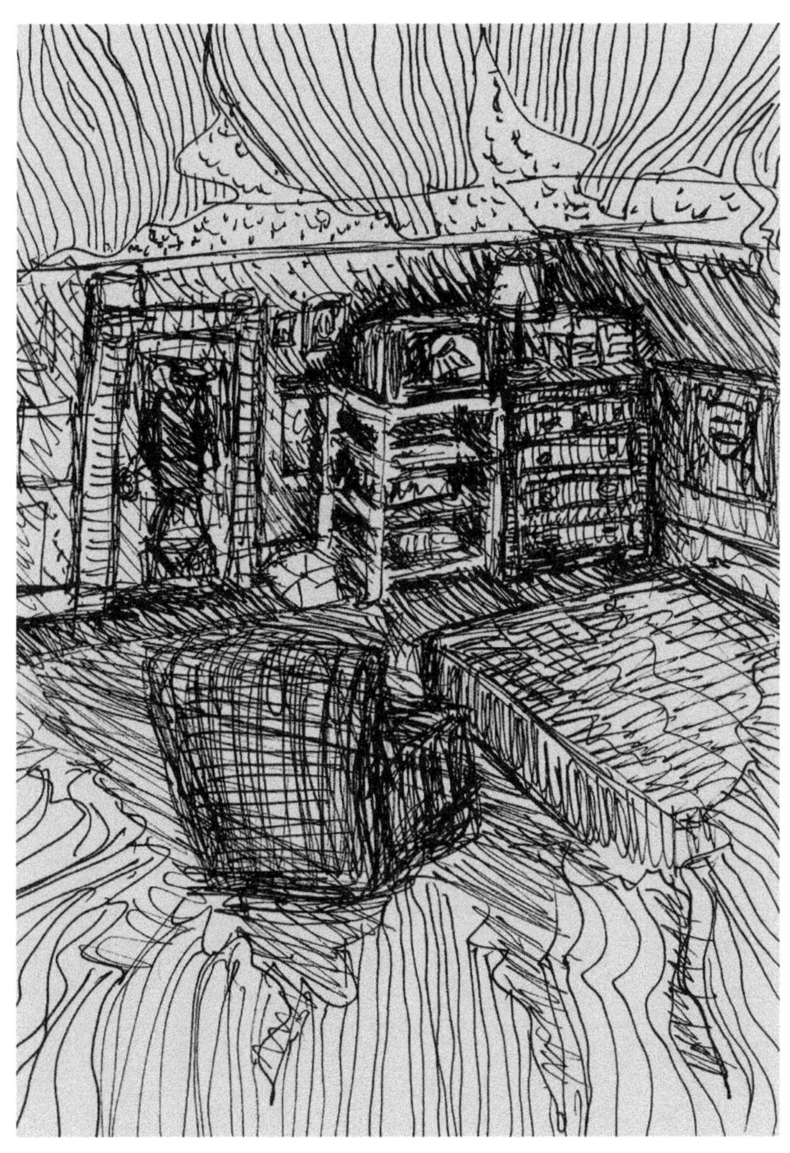

She knew that the details of his room
were eroding
in her mind's eye.

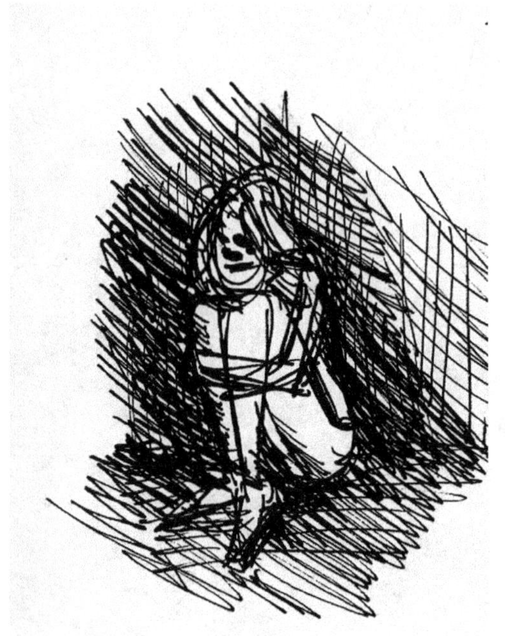

Hug yourself.

Breathe.

Let these memories relax.

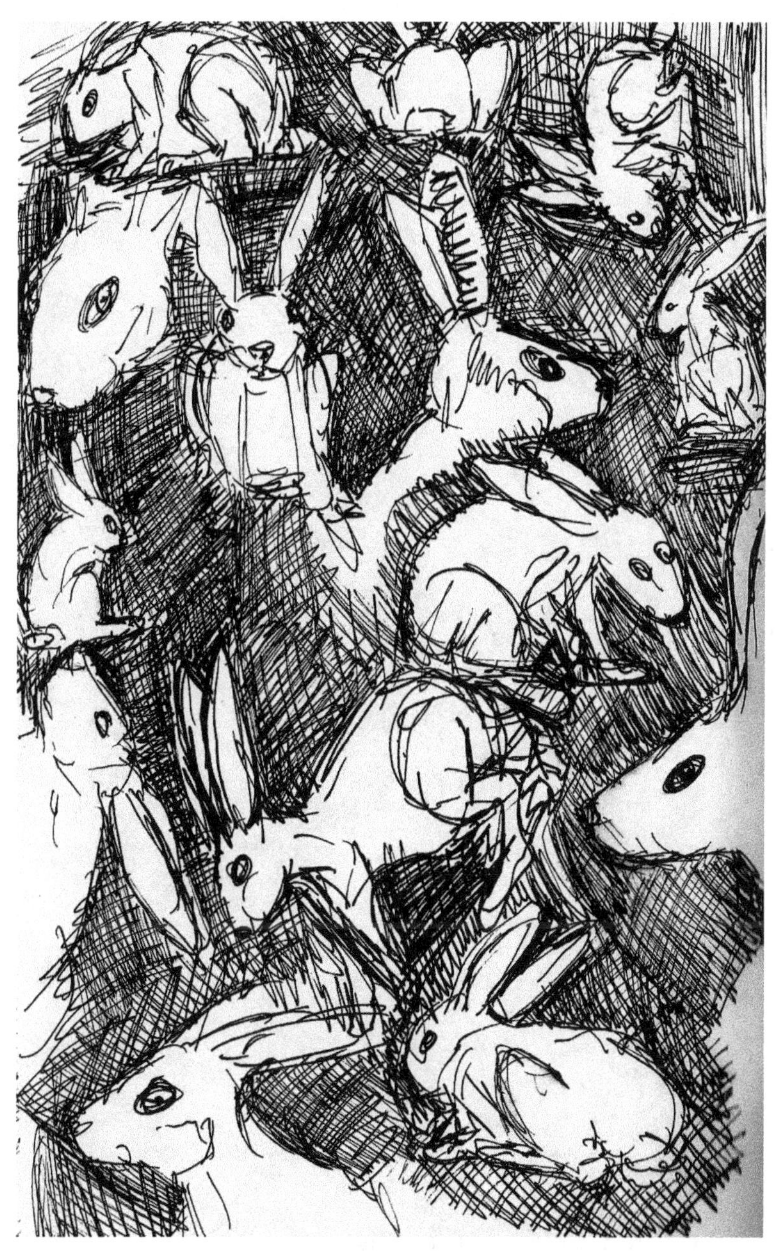

Find peace in repetition.

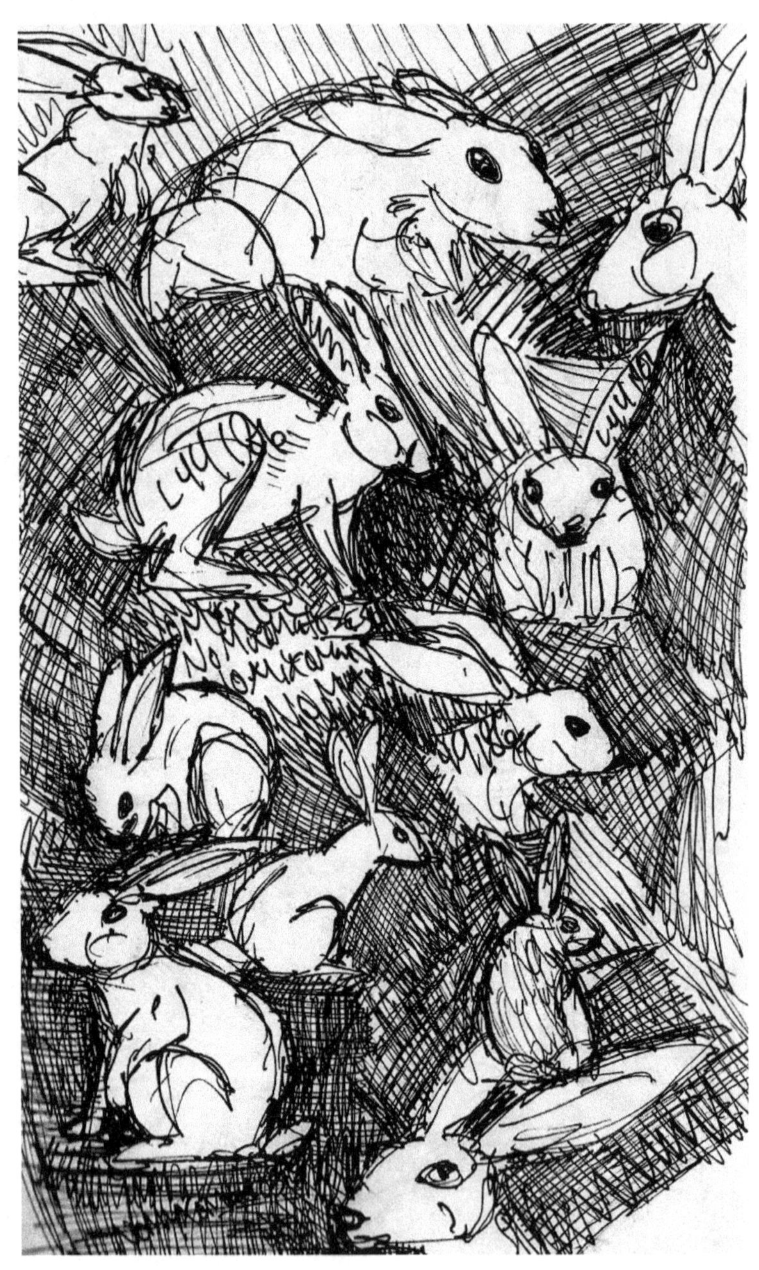

Find truth in repetition.

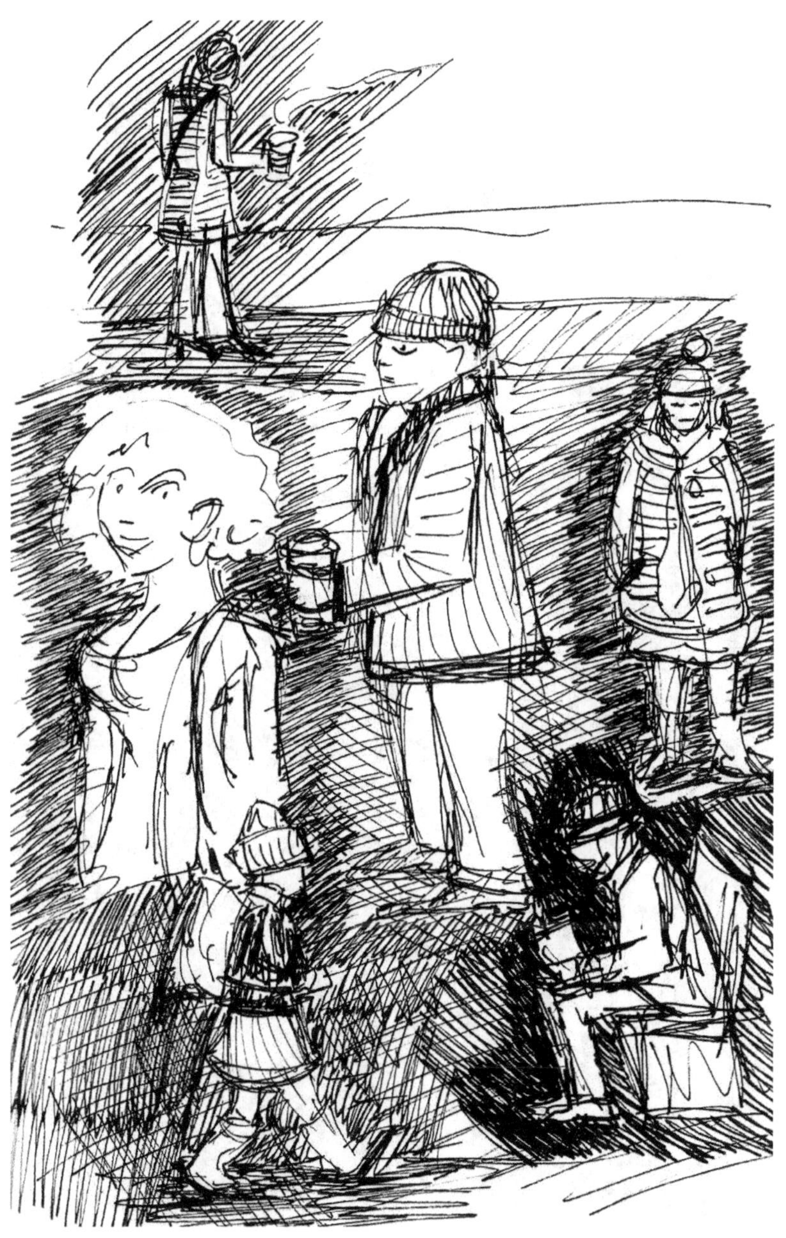

Look until you see who the liars are.

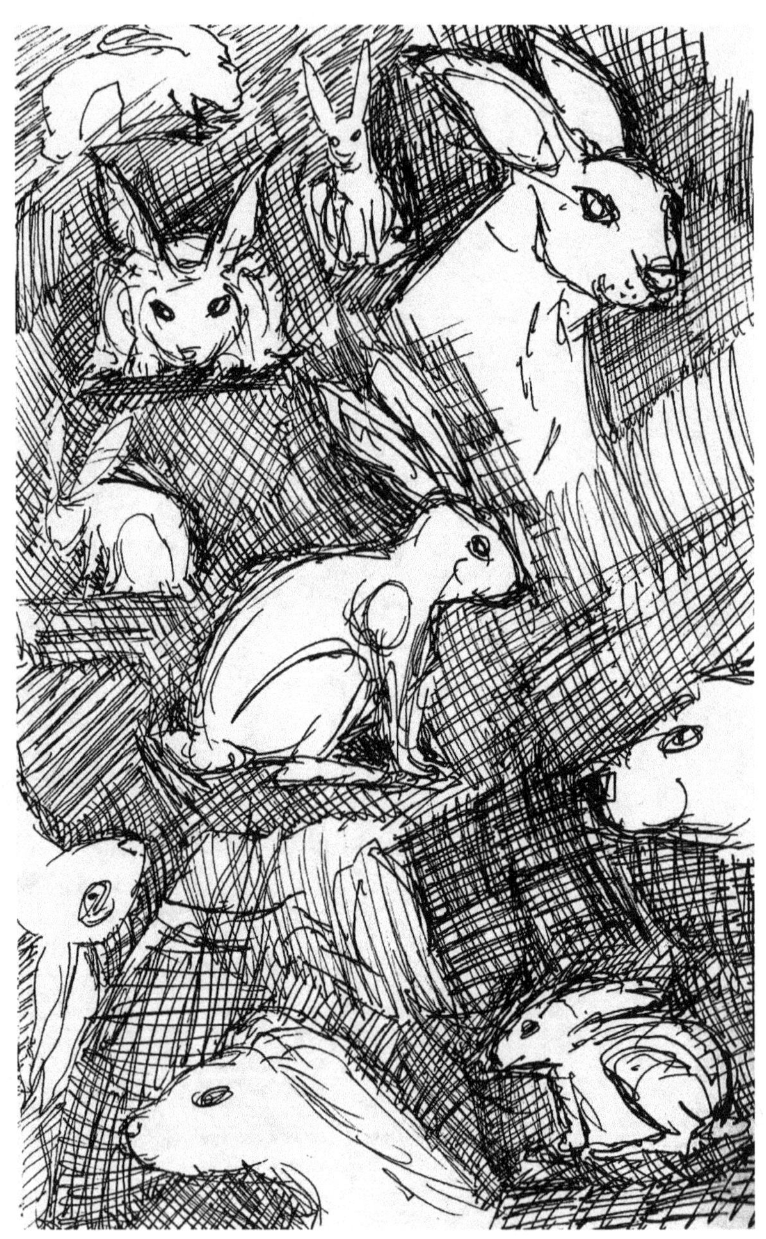

Busy reflections and infinite angles.

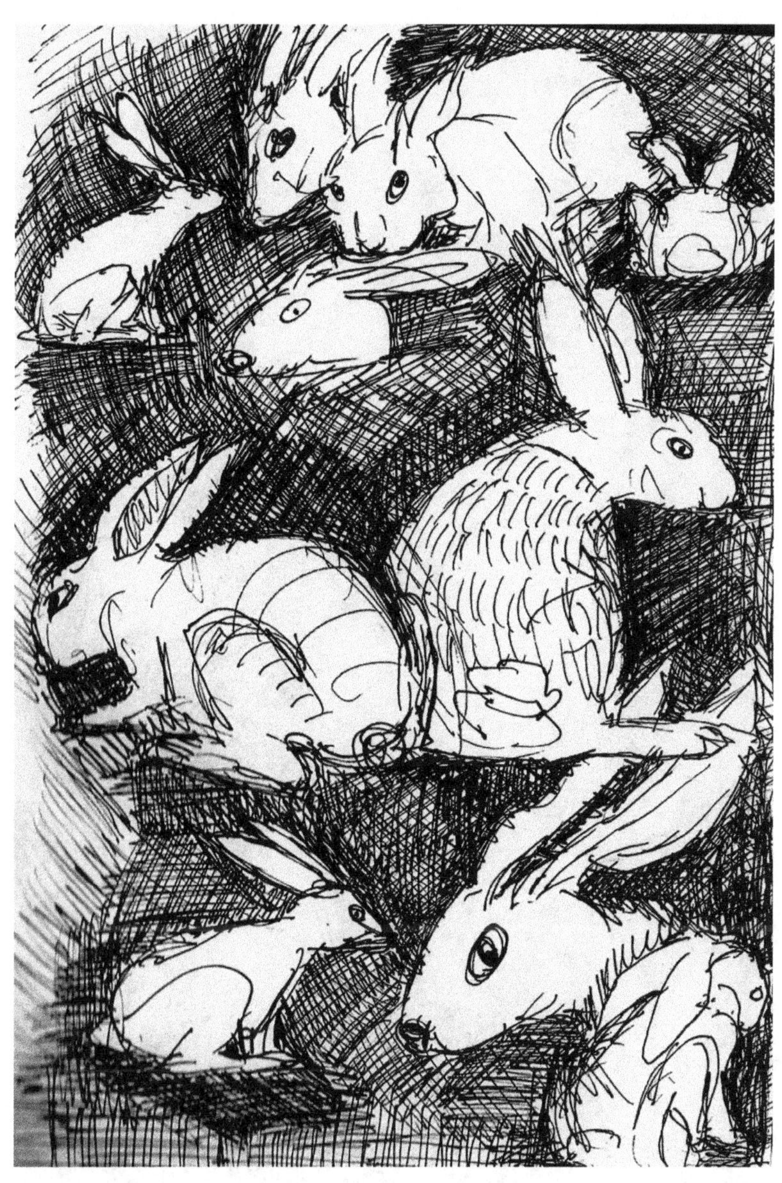

Fixating on the lives of single creatures
helped her forget
the condition of life as a whole.

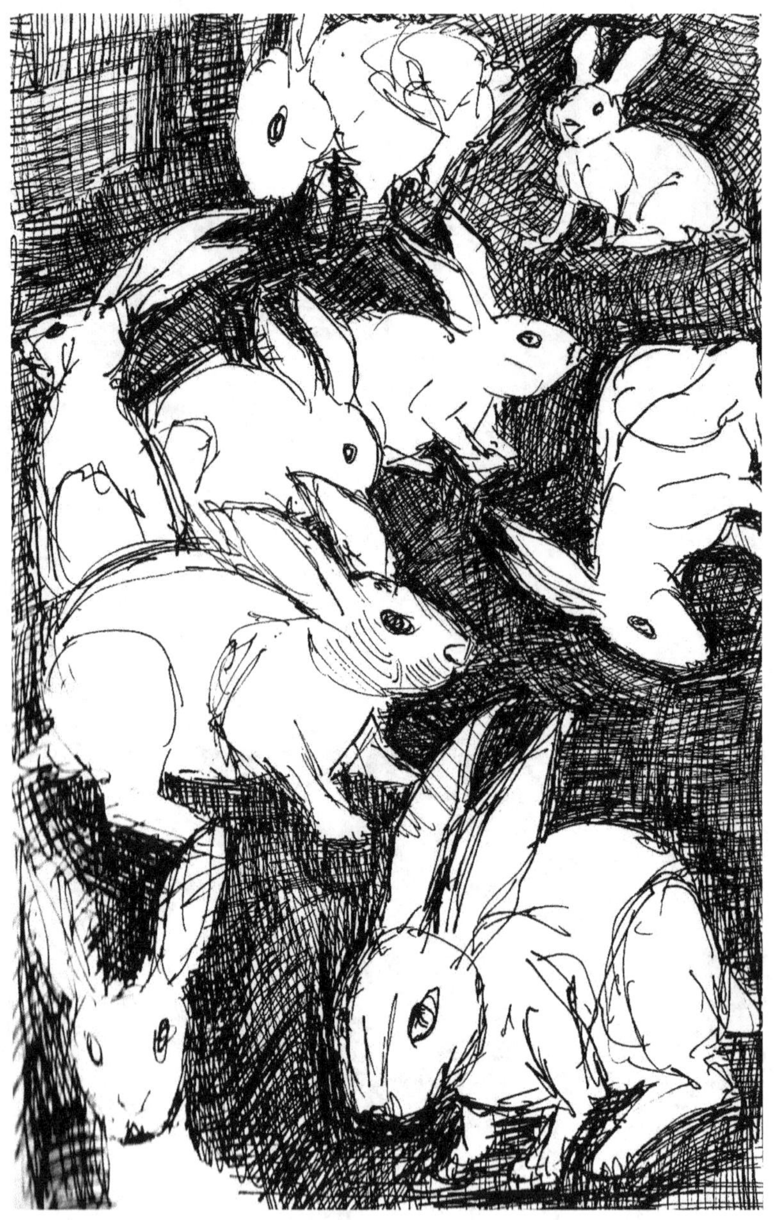

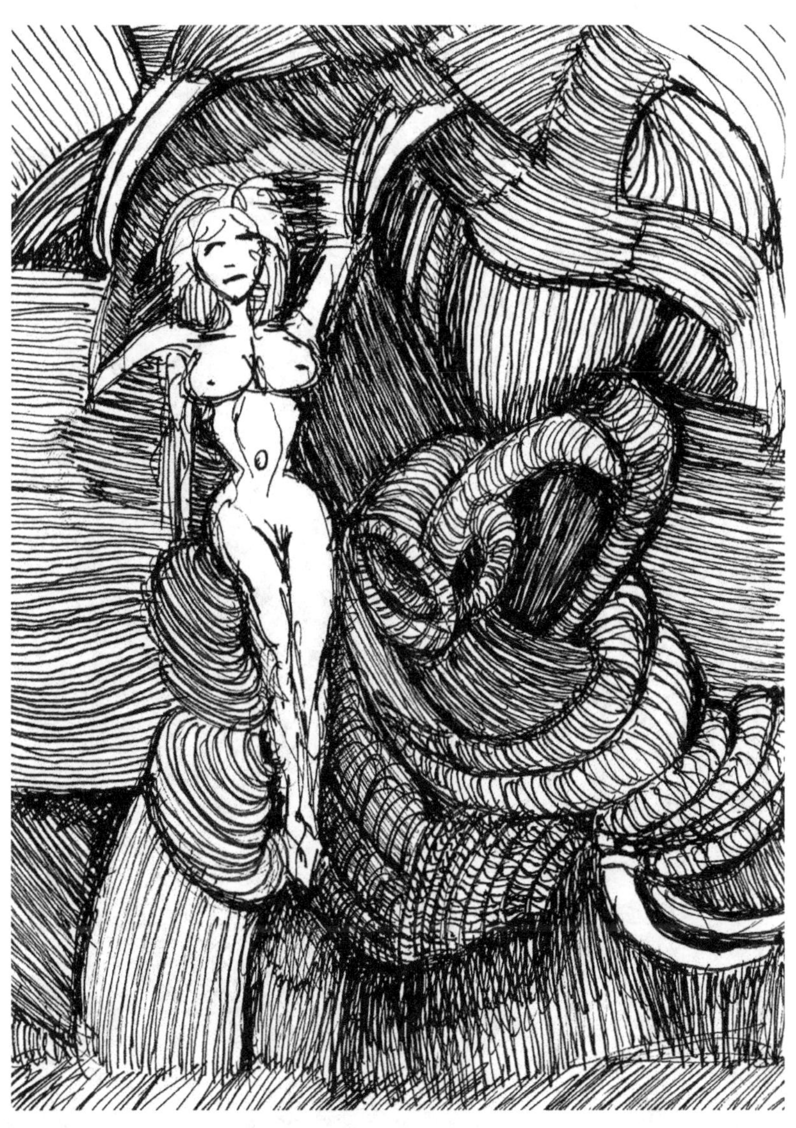

What she saw
when she closed her eyes
was not what drove her.
It was what she felt.

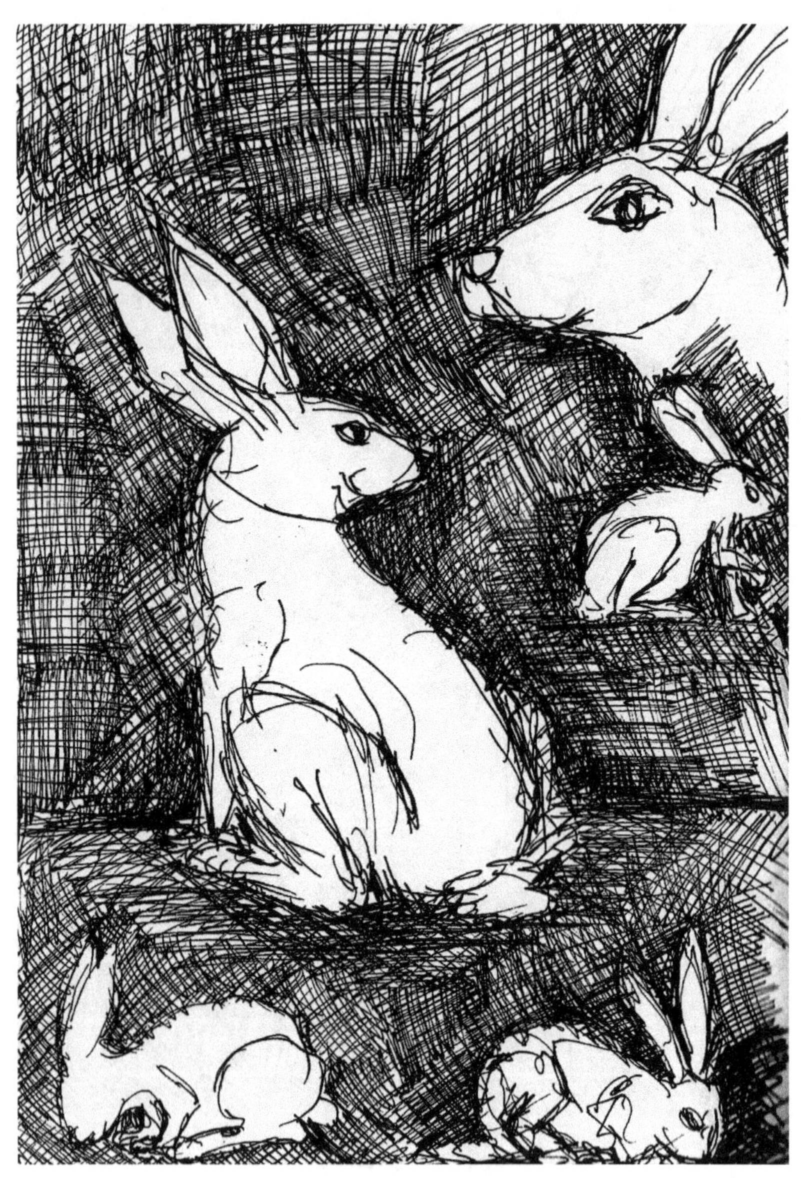

You can know an animal's thoughts
if you immerse yourself
in that animal's actions.

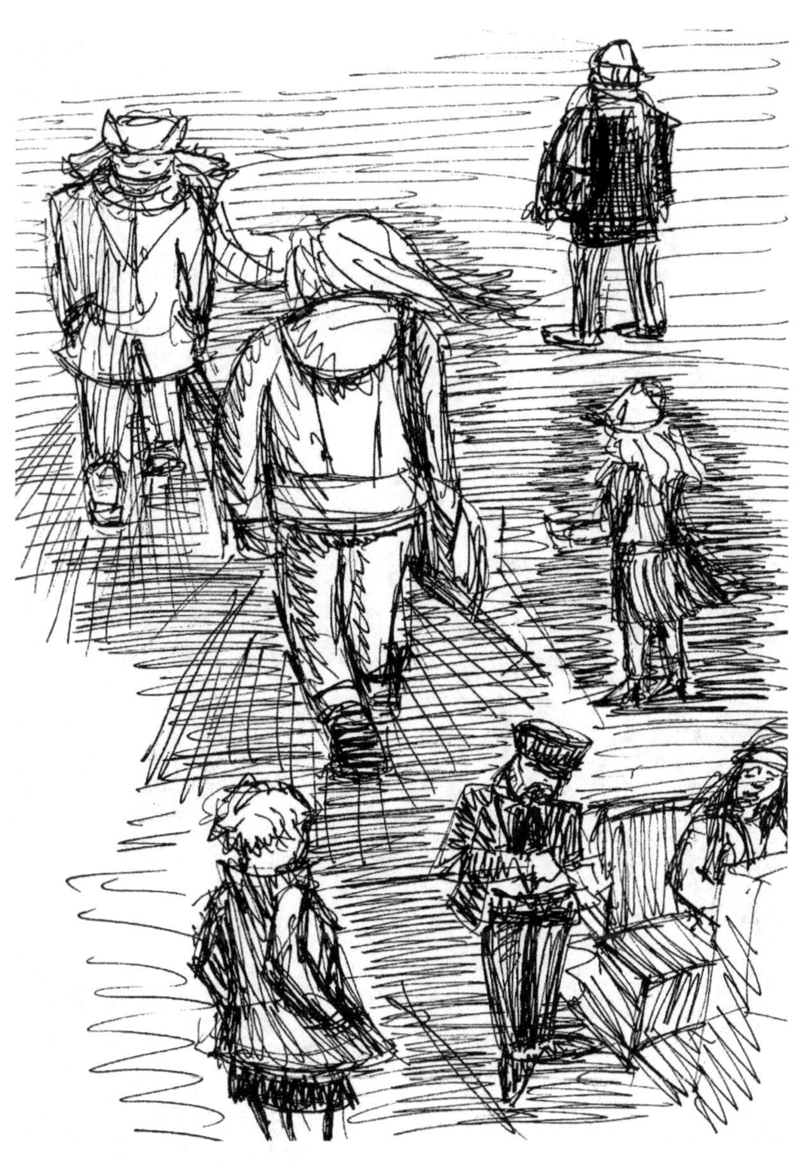

You can know the thoughts of people
if you immerse yourself
in their actions.

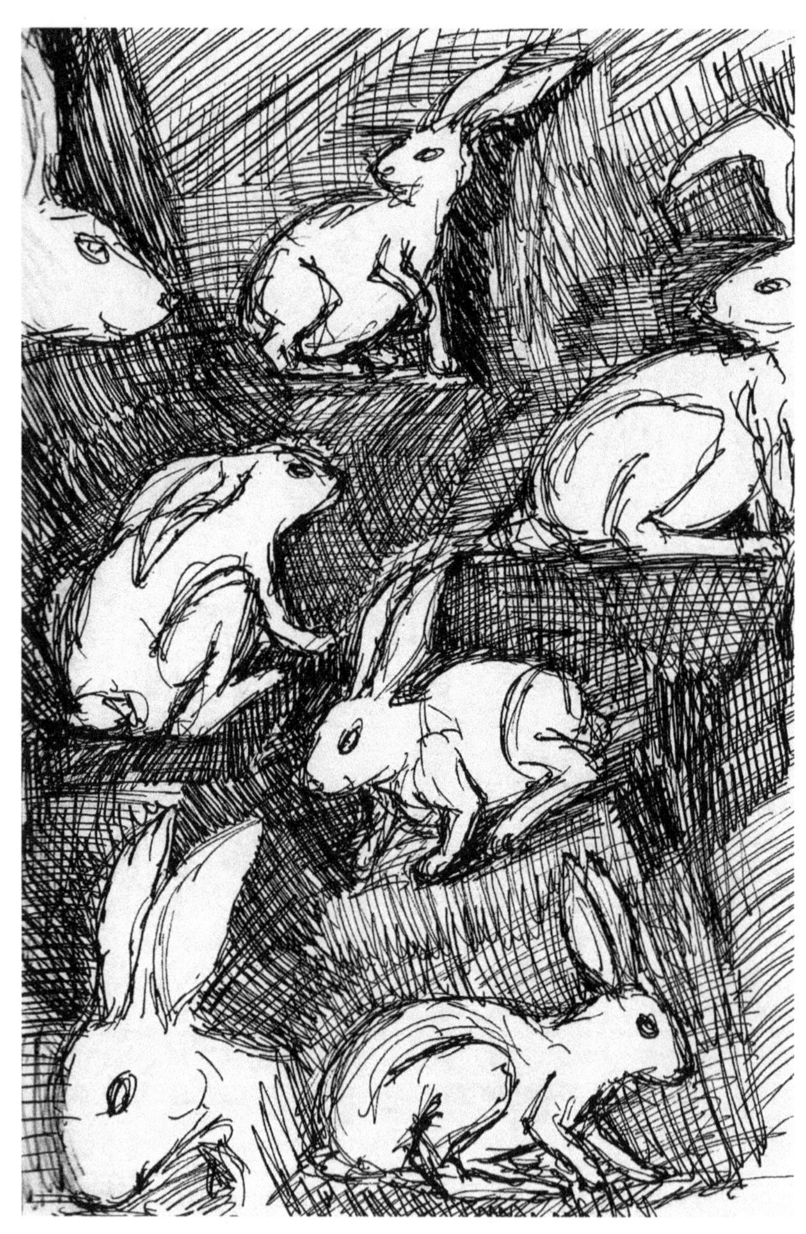

She never saw a rabbit at peace
because she only saw them above ground.

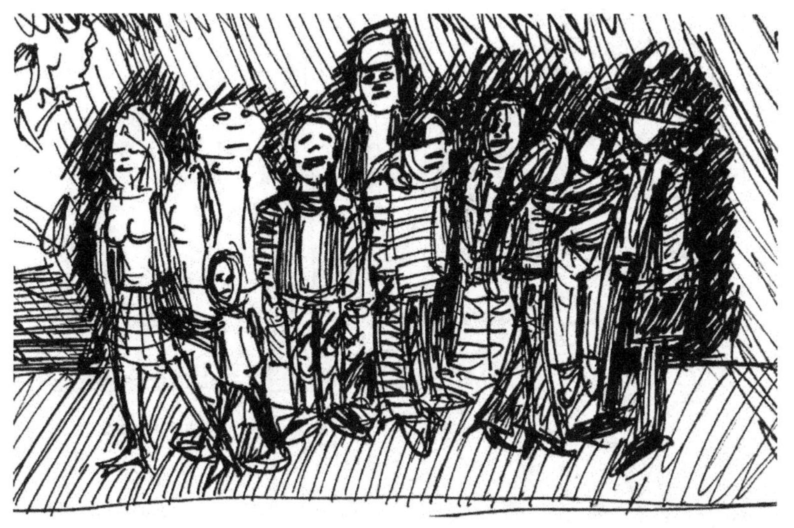

Sometimes

she'd look at a group

and imagine

which of them
would take charge

in a crisis.

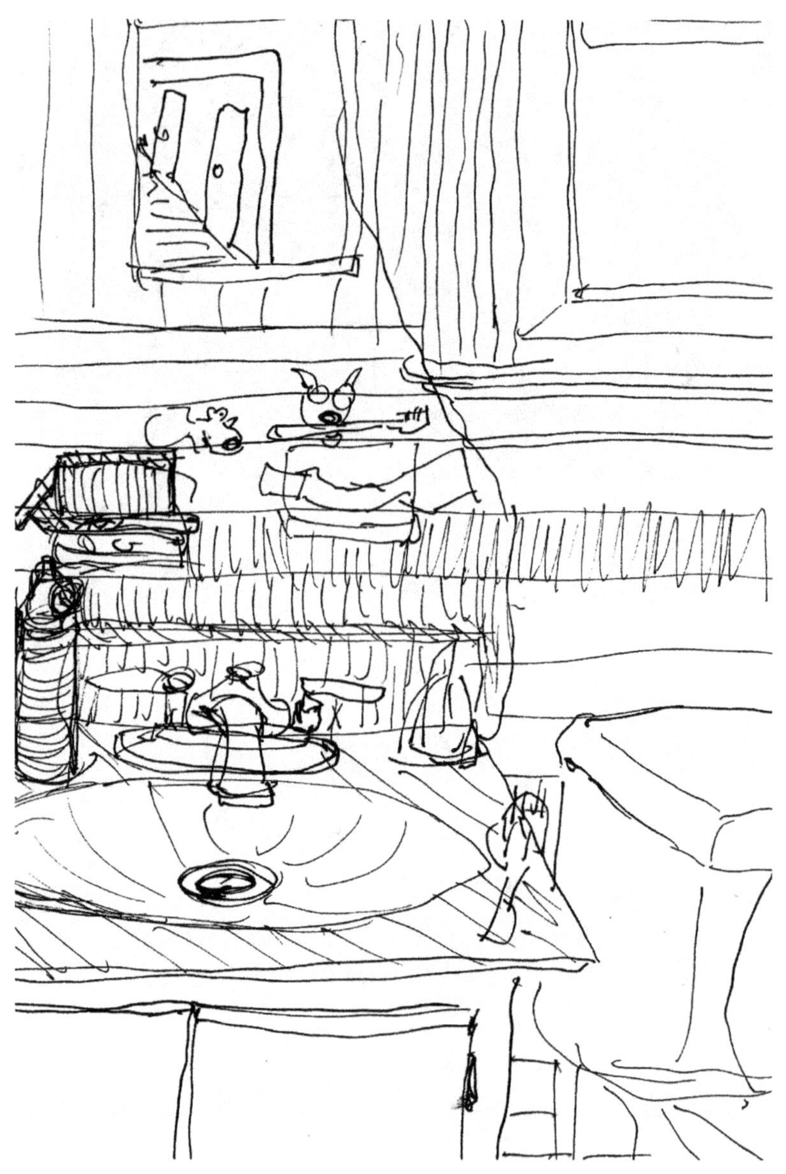

He had said to her,
"If you have a lack of answers from me
it's because I have a lack of questions from you."

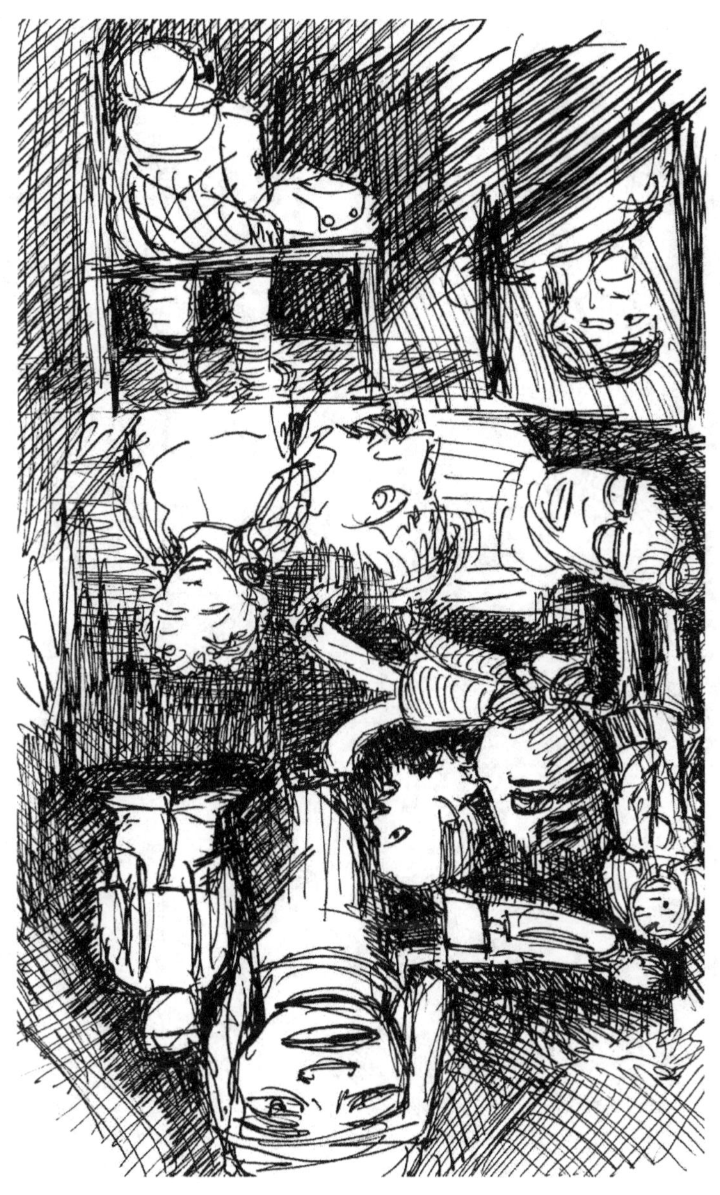

You get what you pay for.
That's why freedom is painful for outcasts.

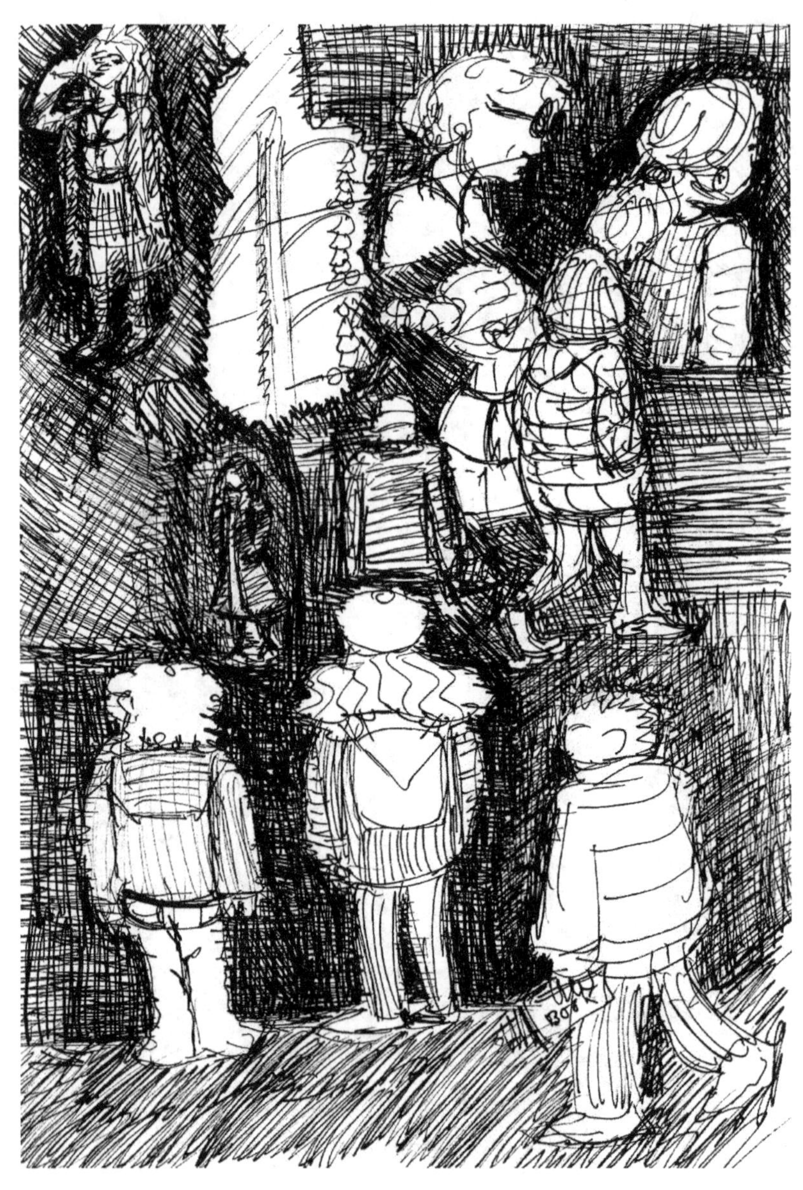

Were strangers turning their backs
to her
more often now?

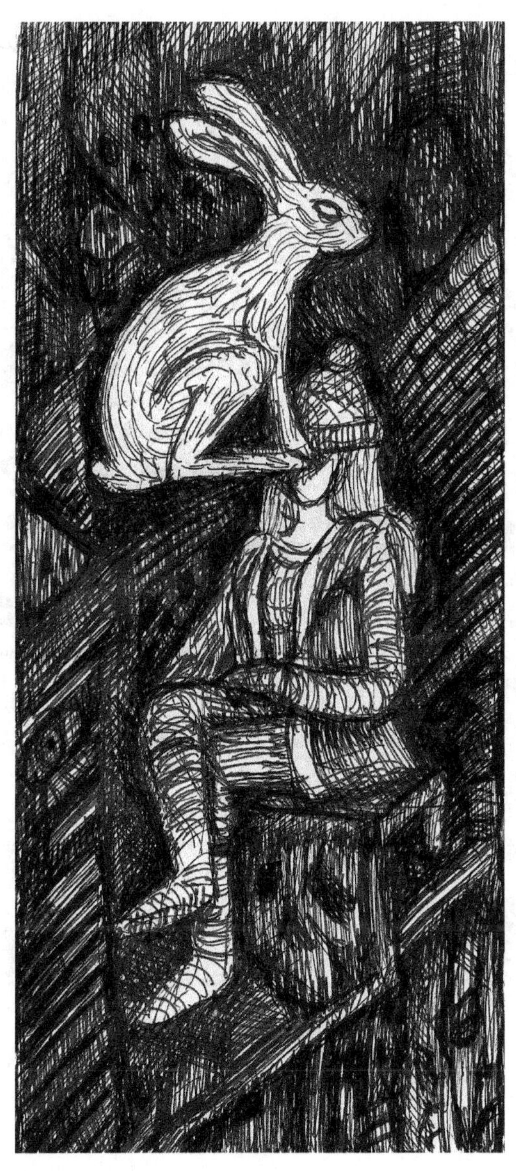

What waking nightmare was this
when all dreams not only drowned
but also became mockeries of who she was?

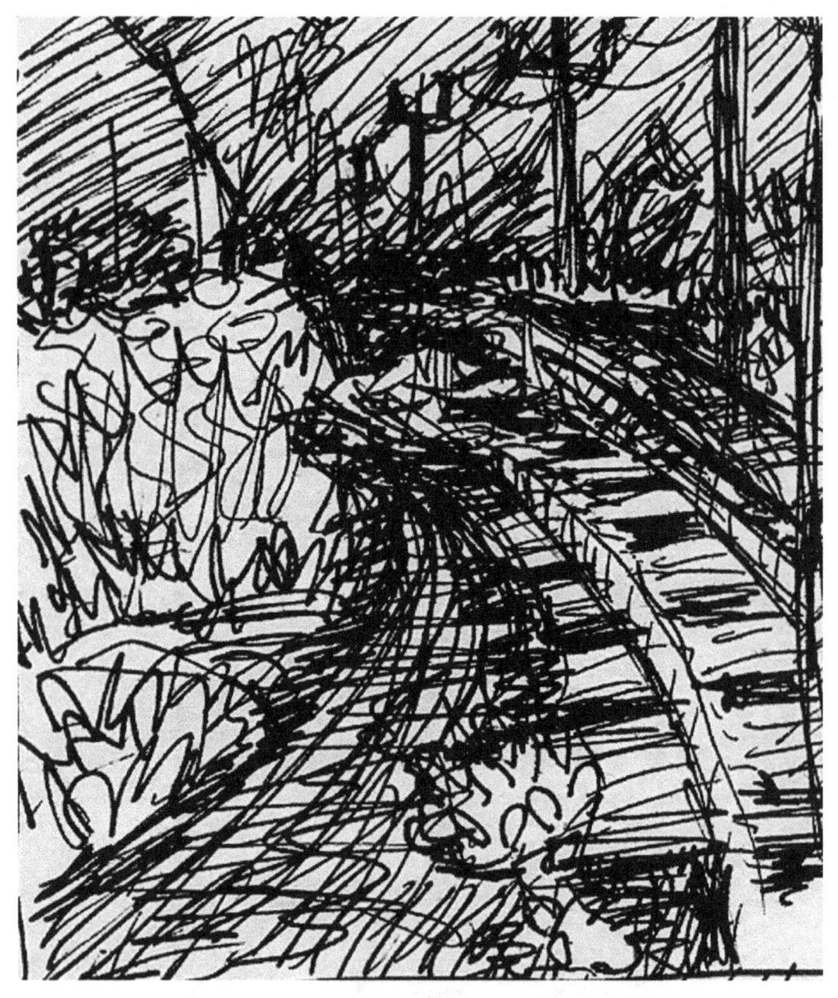

Find the line of the horizon.

Go to it.

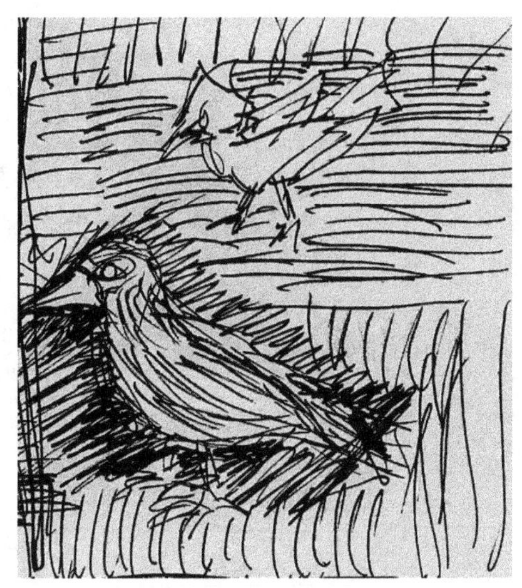

It is not enough

to dream of flying

like a bird.

A true spirit

will also imagine landing.

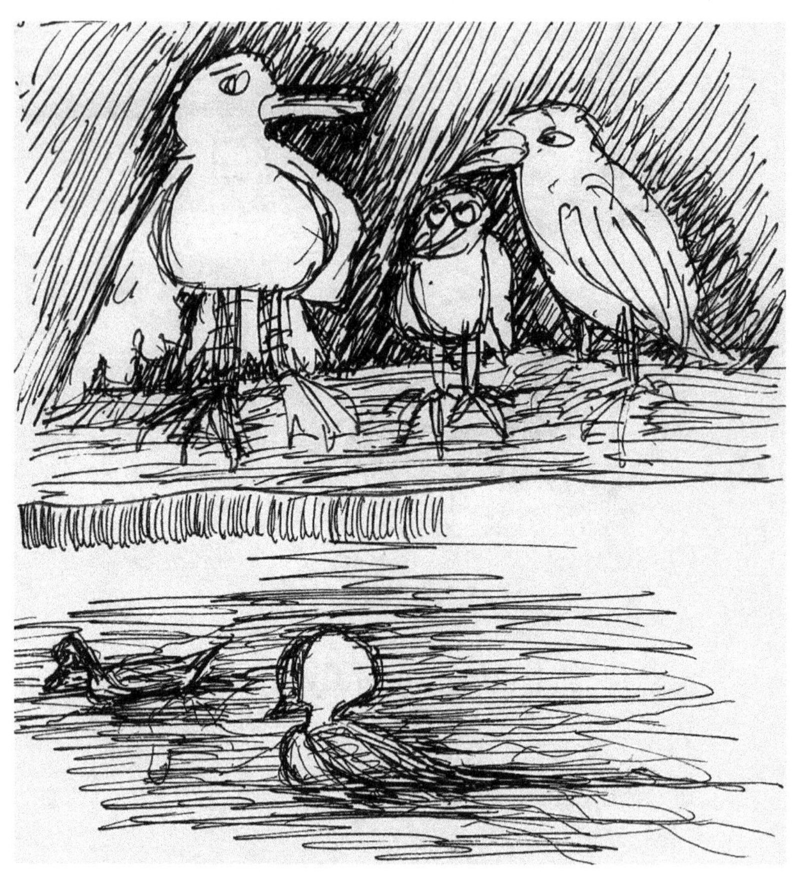

She realized

birds do not make eye contact.

It changed how she thought of them.

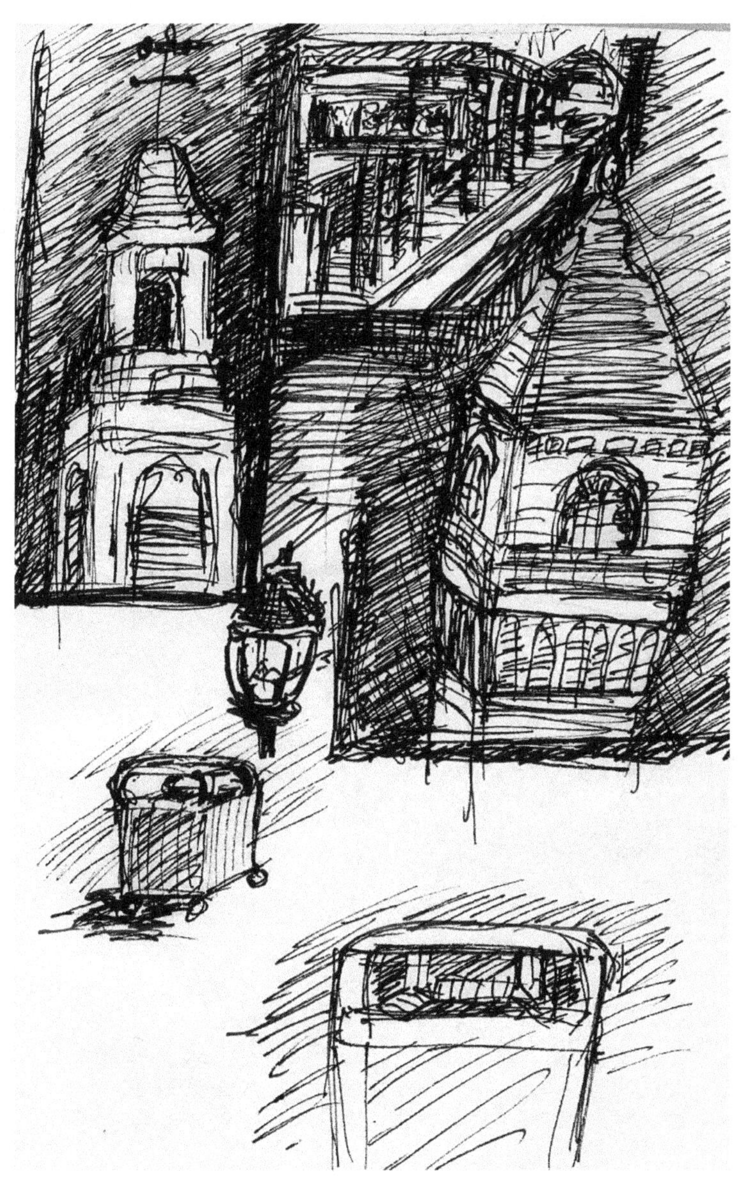

Vertigo at every height.

Vertigo at every sight.

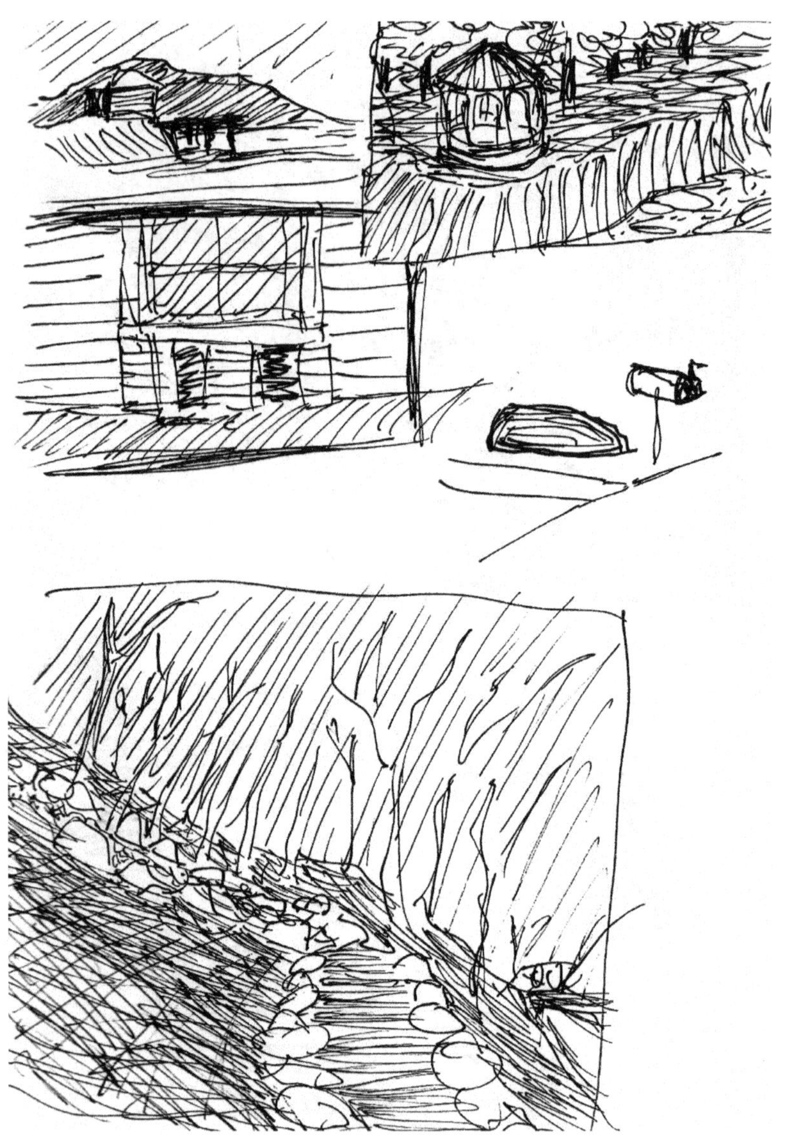

Buildings and objects do what people do.
They wait and wait
for use, occupation and destruction.

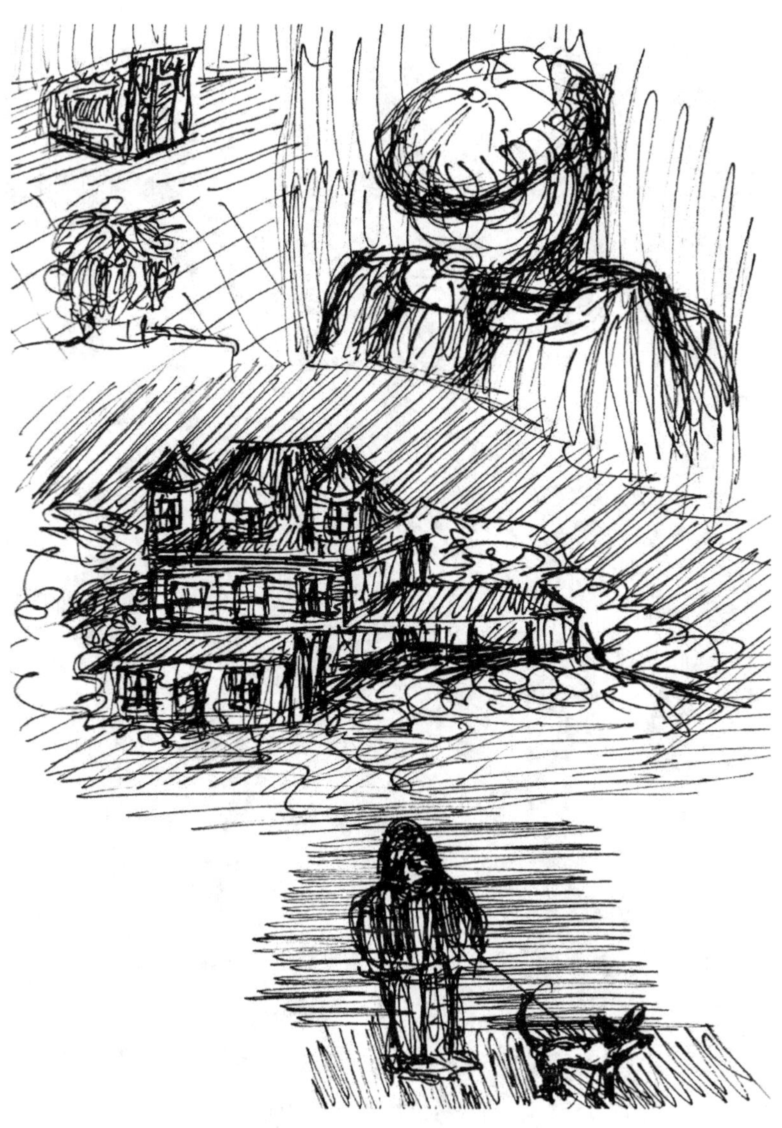

Her eyes were always focused
on something that was not there.
She began to realize
she did not want a life of waiting.

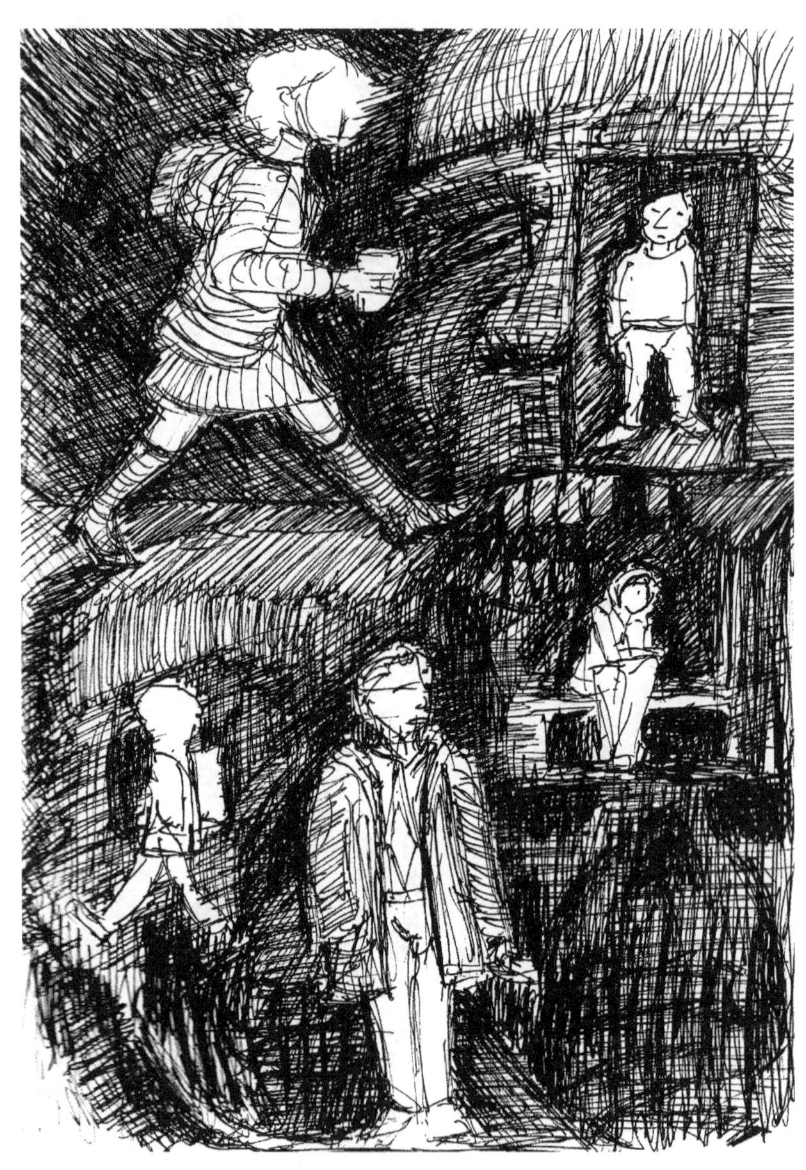

"Come back to this world,"
she told herself.
"Come back to what is before you."

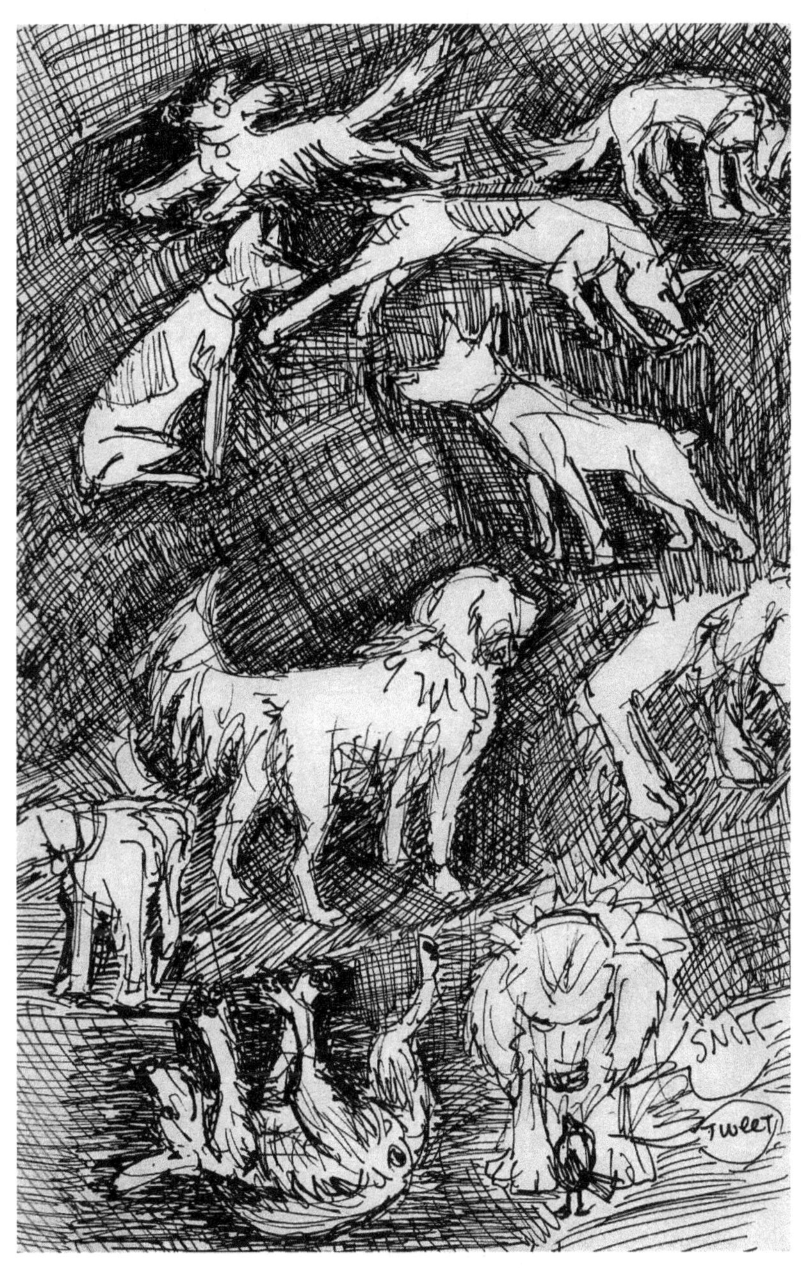


Release.

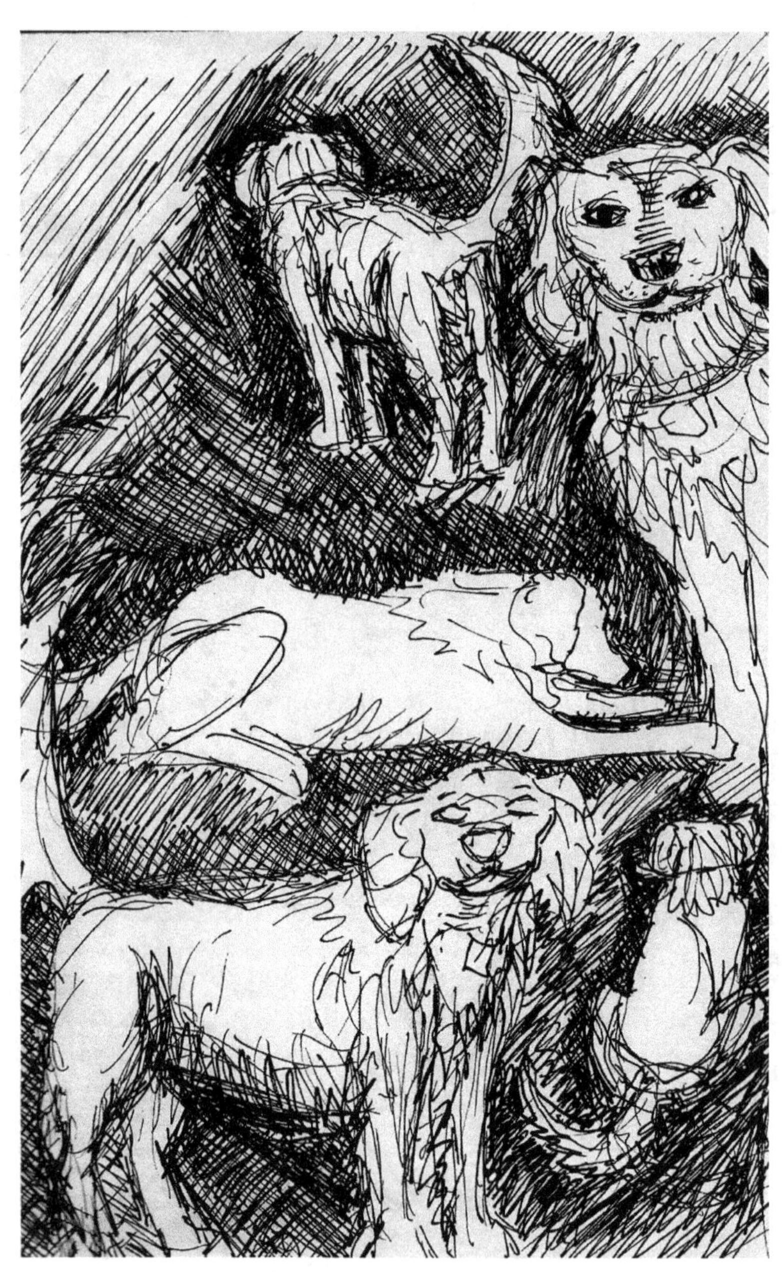

Why hold on to a pride that holds you back?

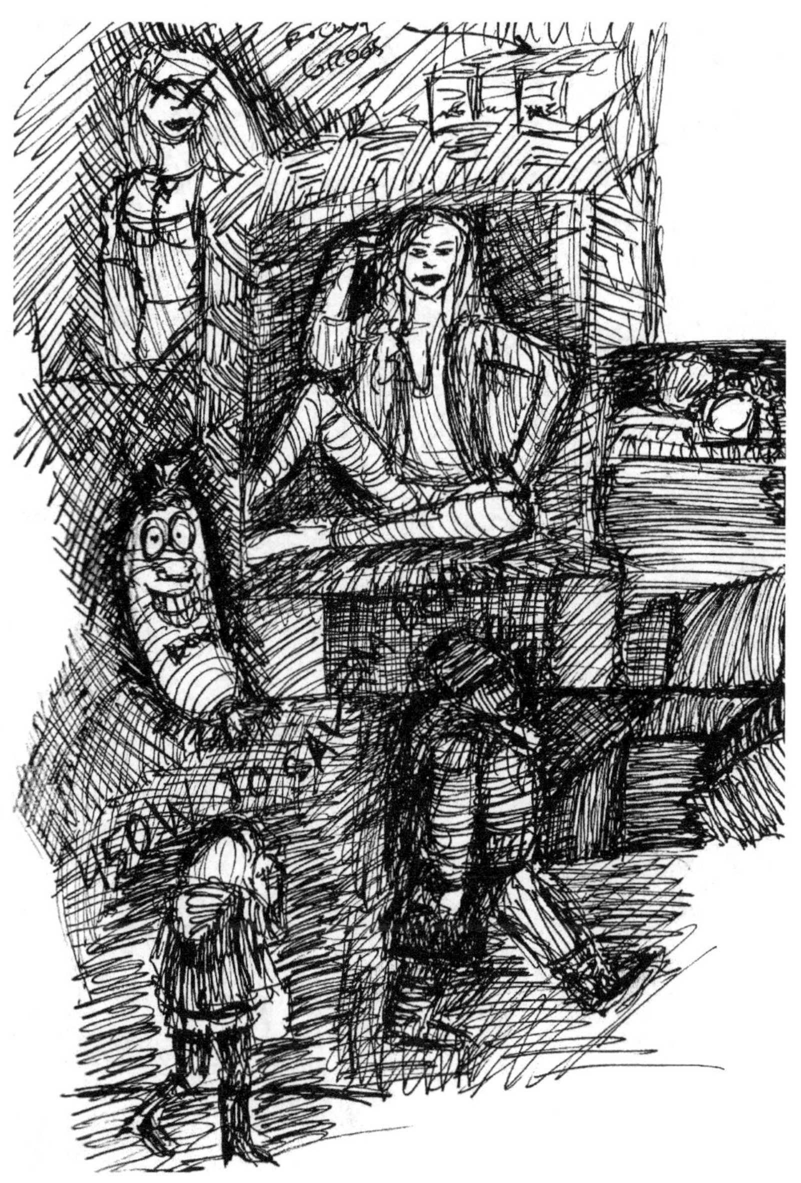

Habit turns contortions into comforts

and then comforts into chains.

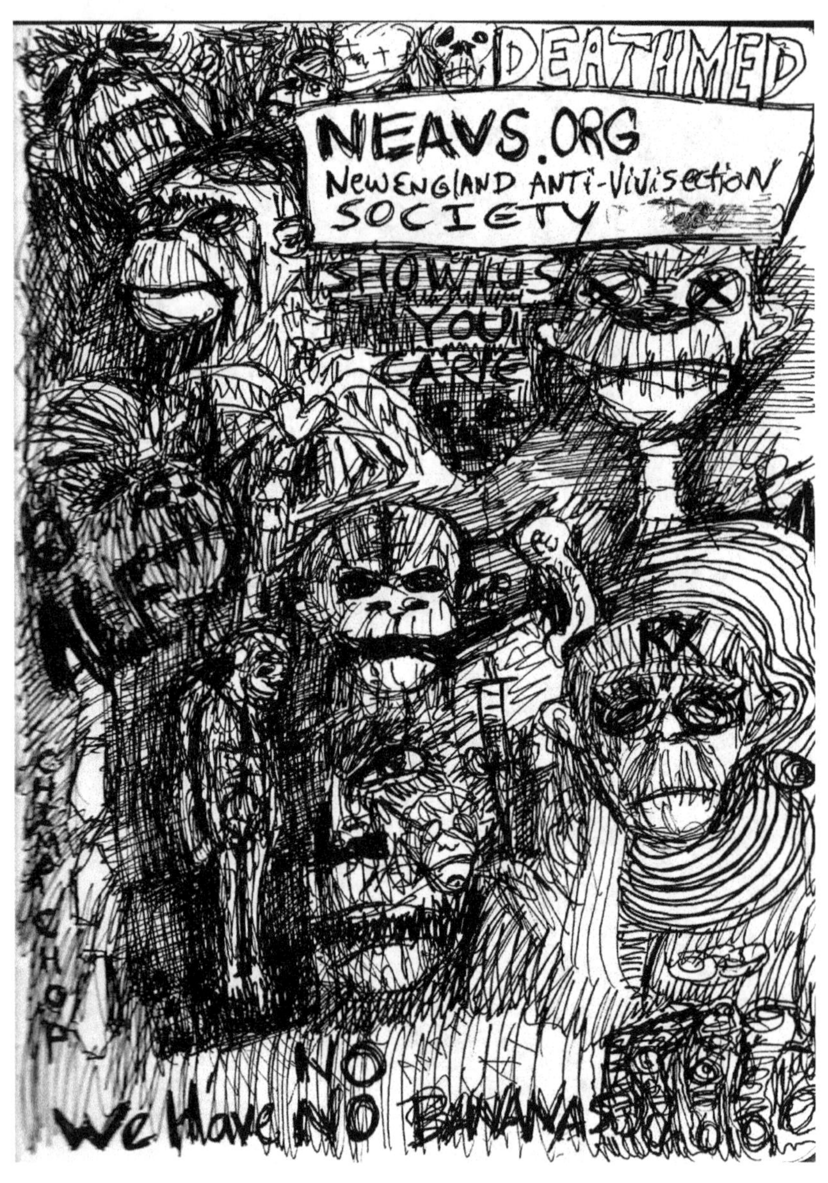


What gets boxed away
will give weight to the box's corners
and corners never fit well in a free-flowing mind.

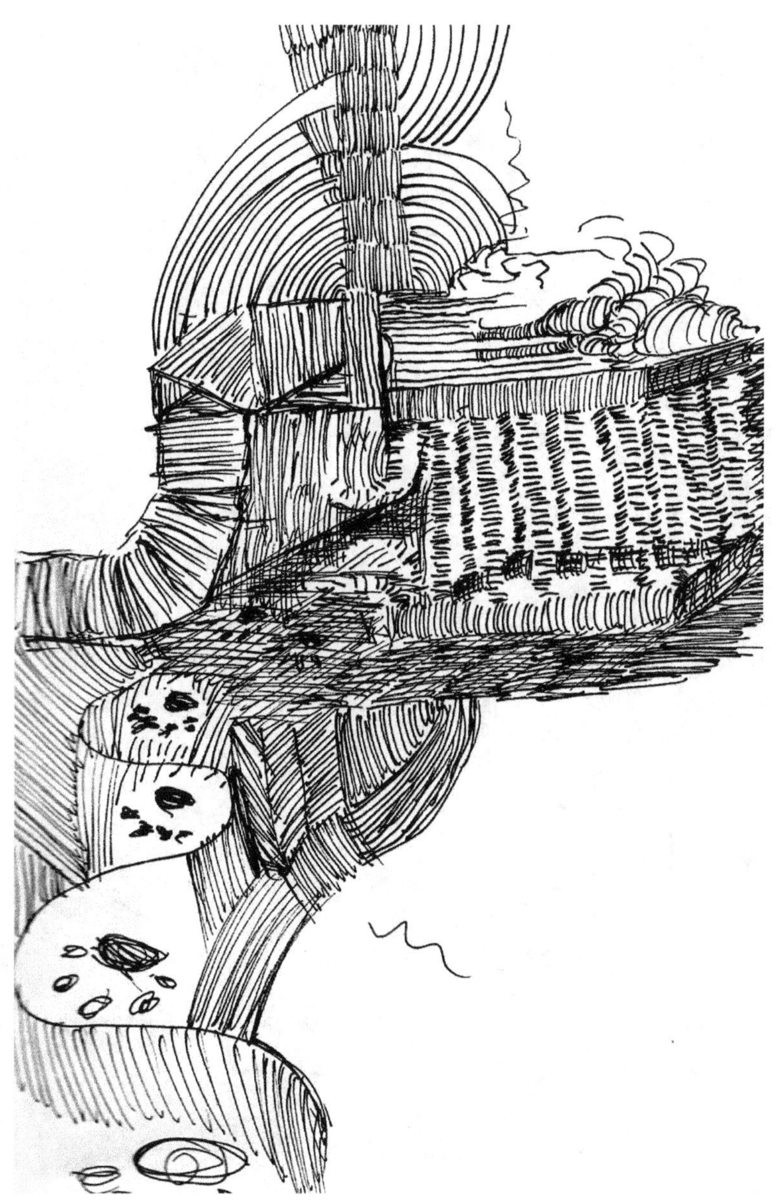

Her vision began to pull her forward.
She saw clear paths in every vista.

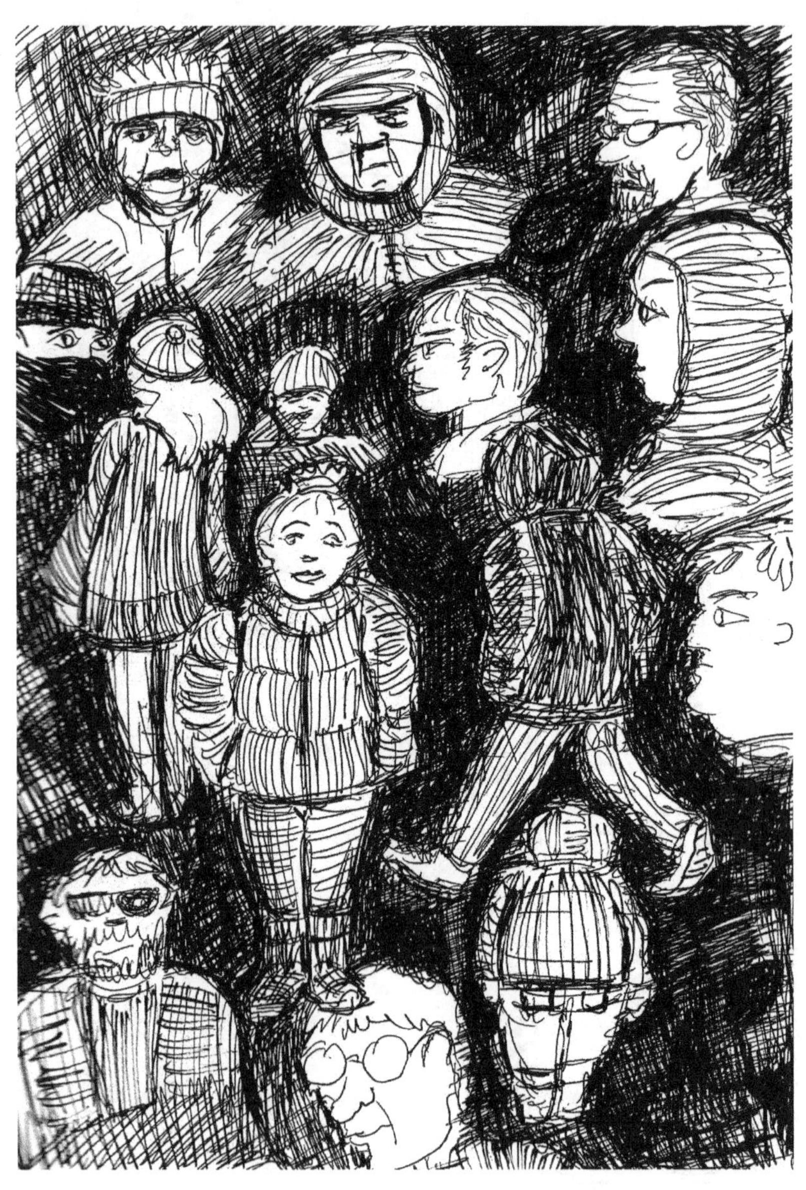

She realized the best way
to know someone is to gauge
how clearly they see their destination.

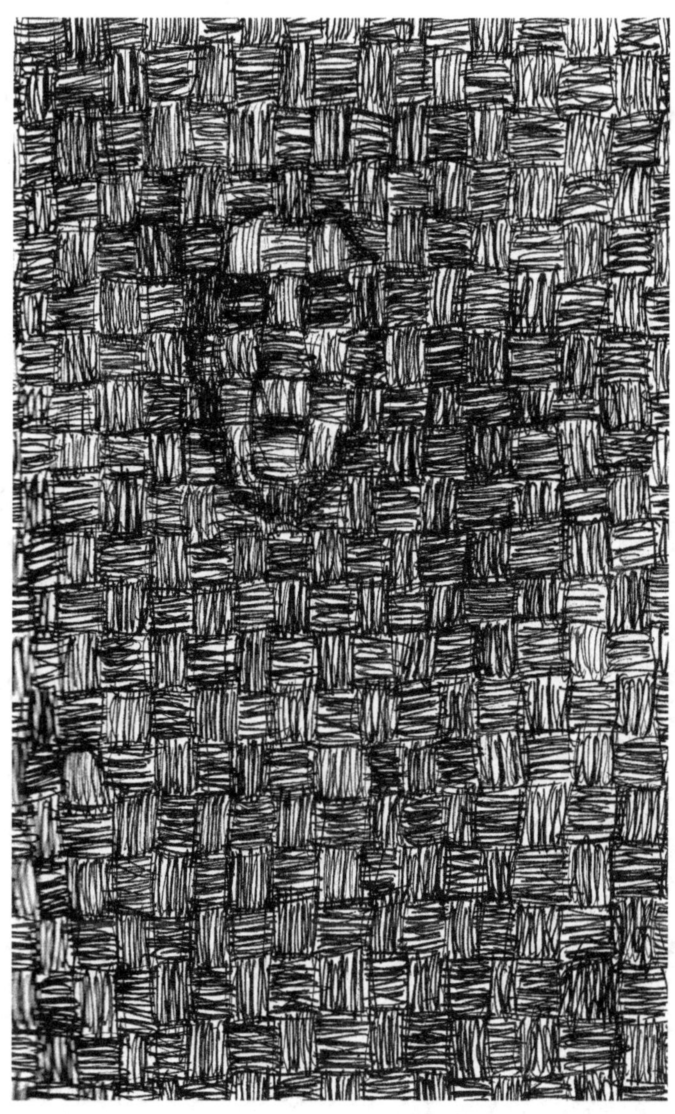

No pattern is without variations.
Controlling the variations is the difference
between mastering patterns
and being mastered by them.

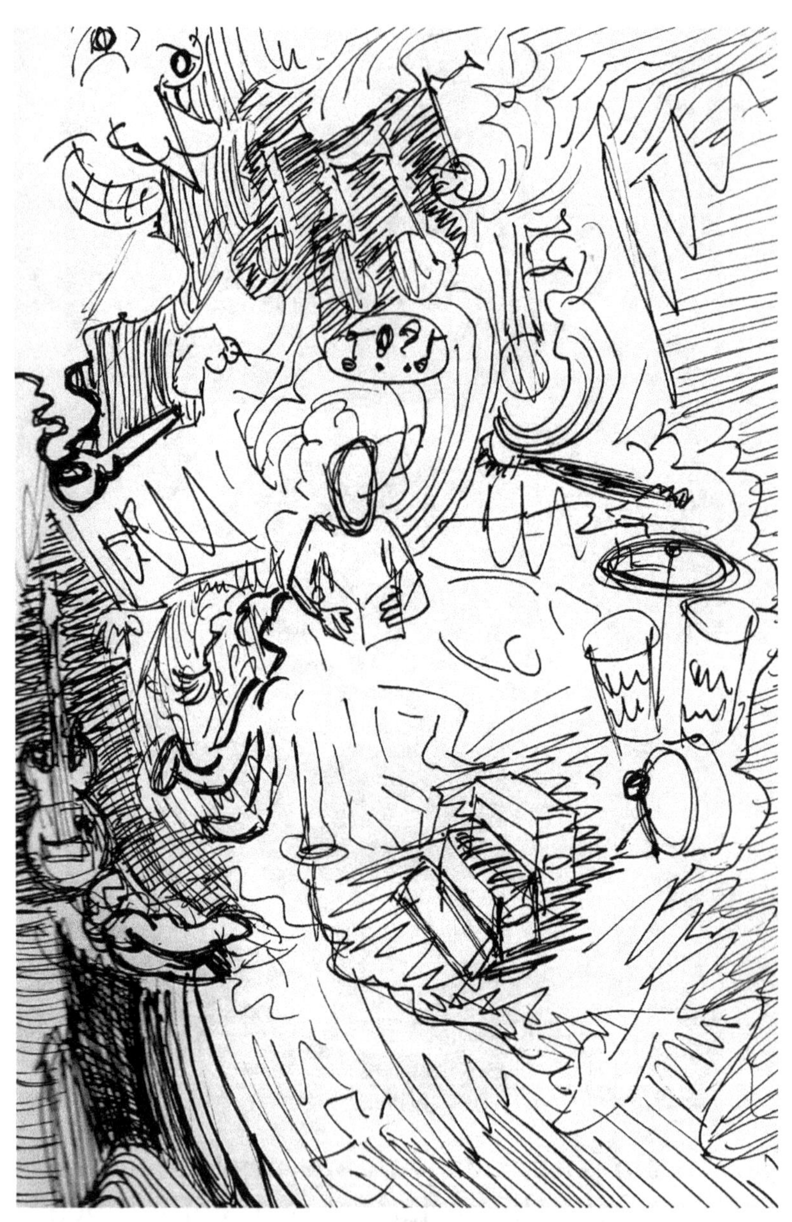

Race to become who you are.

There were fears she carried

but because they were born of experience
she had been calling them wisdom.

She realized the lie in that.

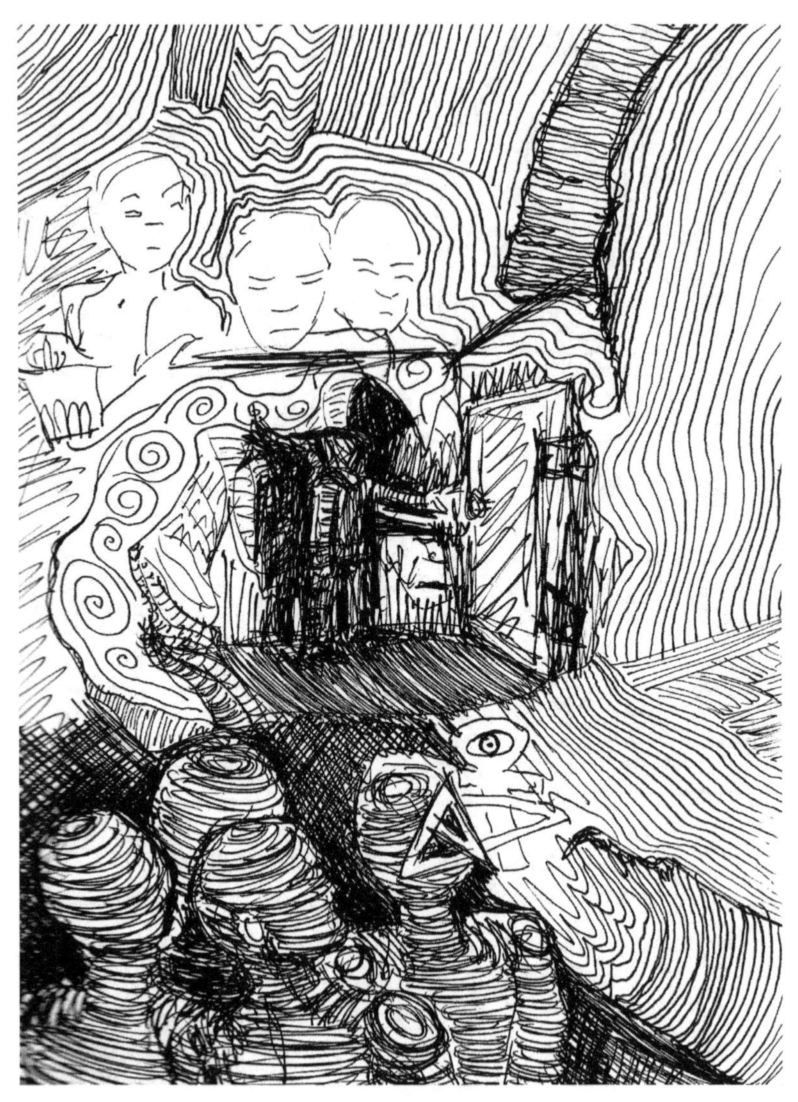

She wondered,

"What if we spoke openly
of all the hypotheticals
we keep to ourselves?"

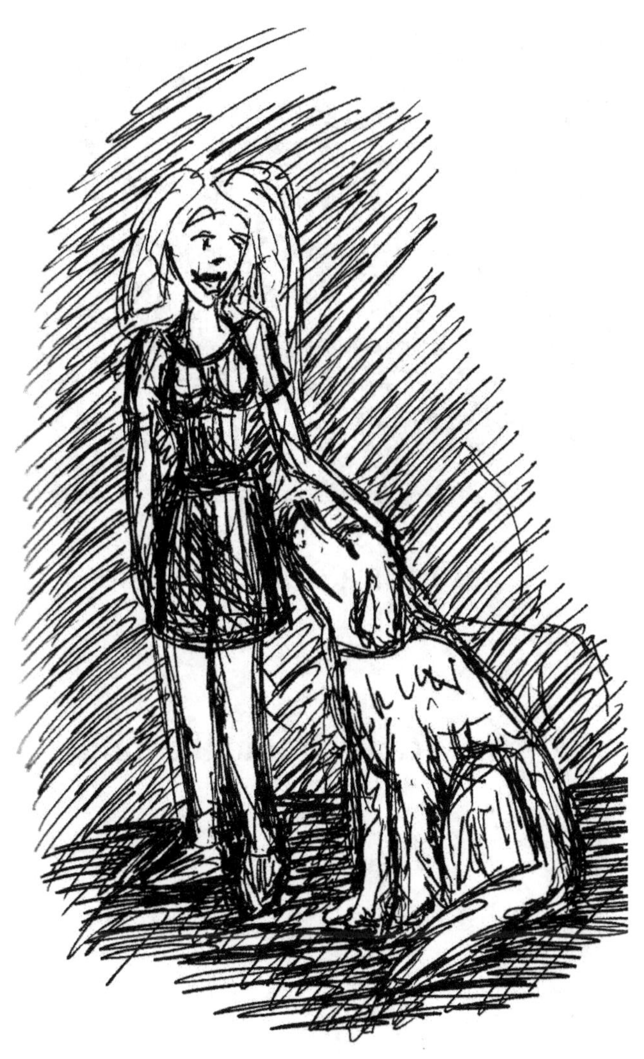

Some give so much credit to training
that they overlook
what came before the training.

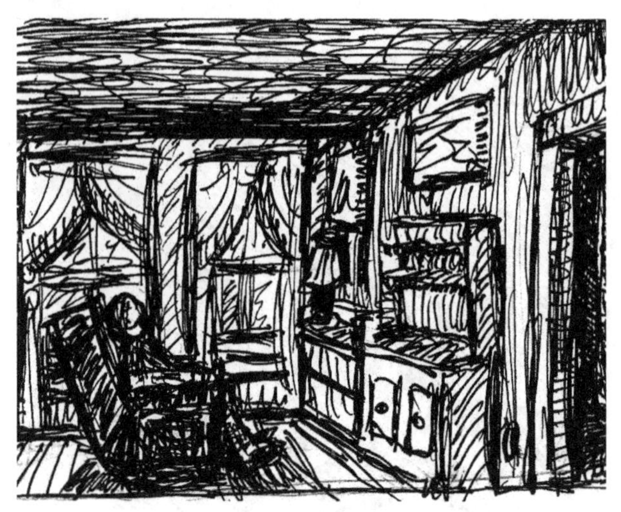

Comfort is a frame of mind

but

comforts can reframe the mind.

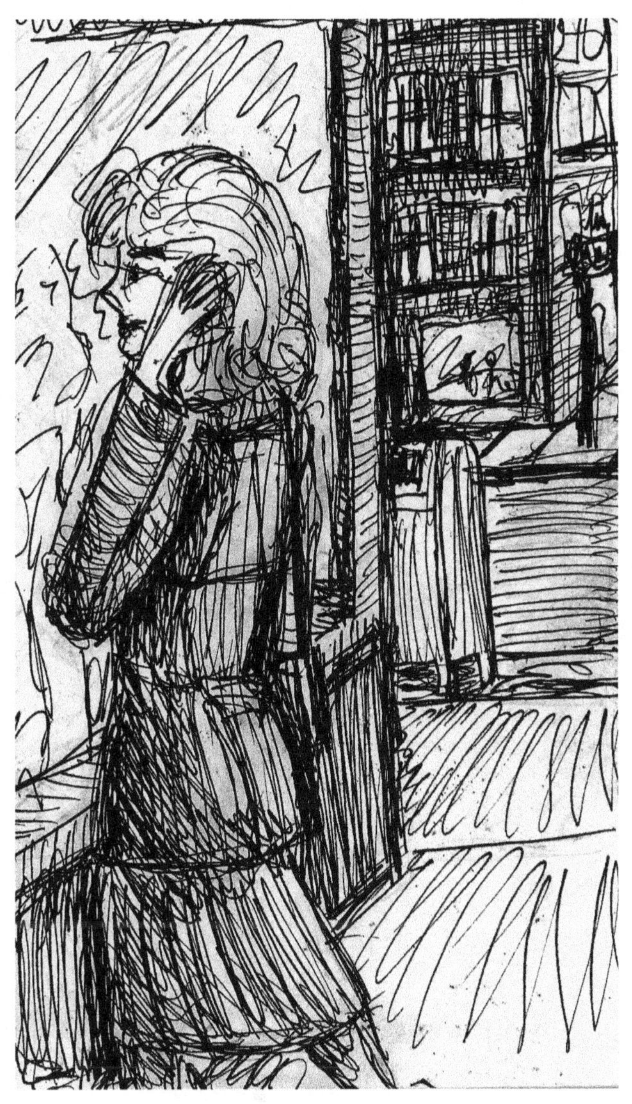

Some feel the need to keep secret
how often they look at their reflection.

Some do not hide it.

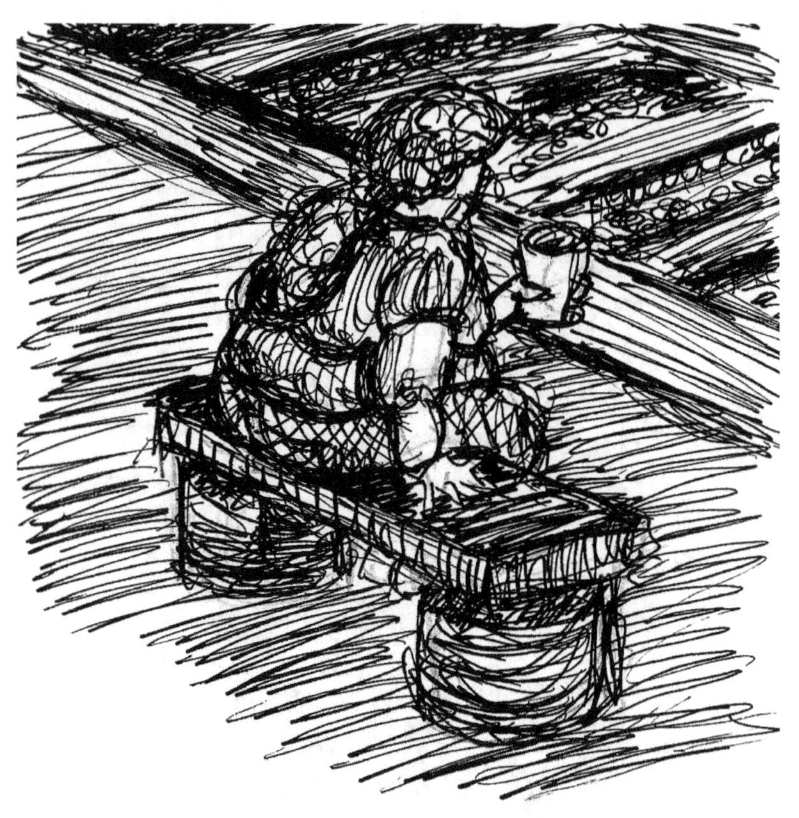

Not everyone who is waiting

is alone

but everyone who is alone

is in some way waiting.

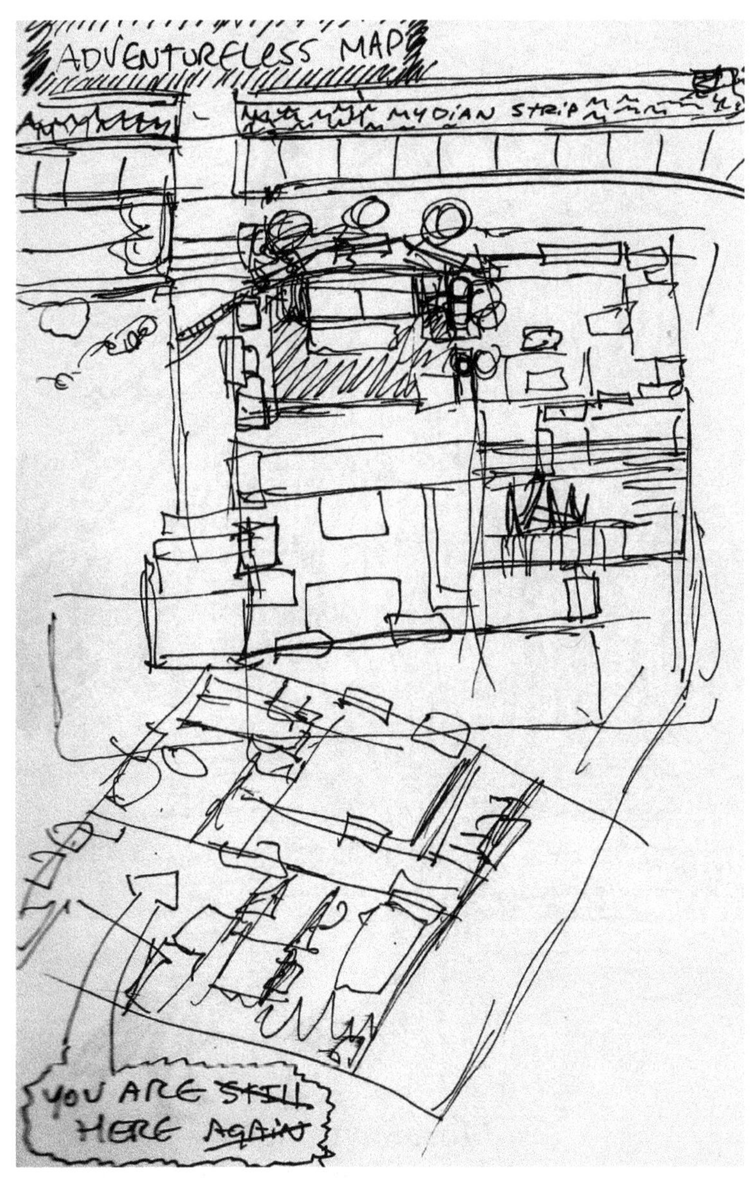


She wondered
how differently she would live life
if she could view her habits from any perspective.

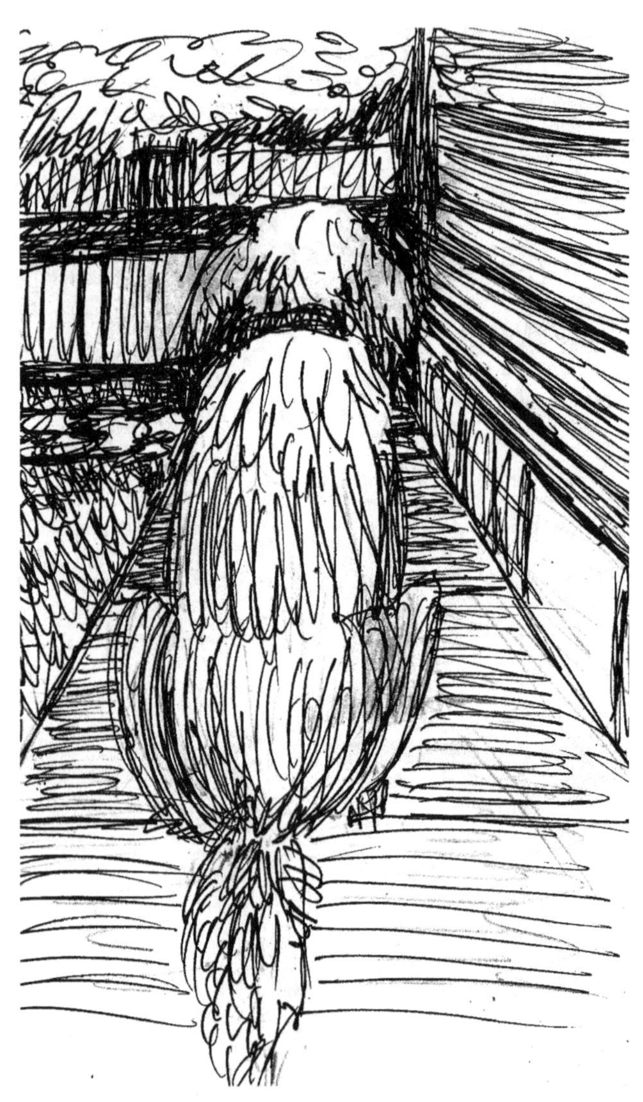

Most anything
can be said to be both
simple and complicated.

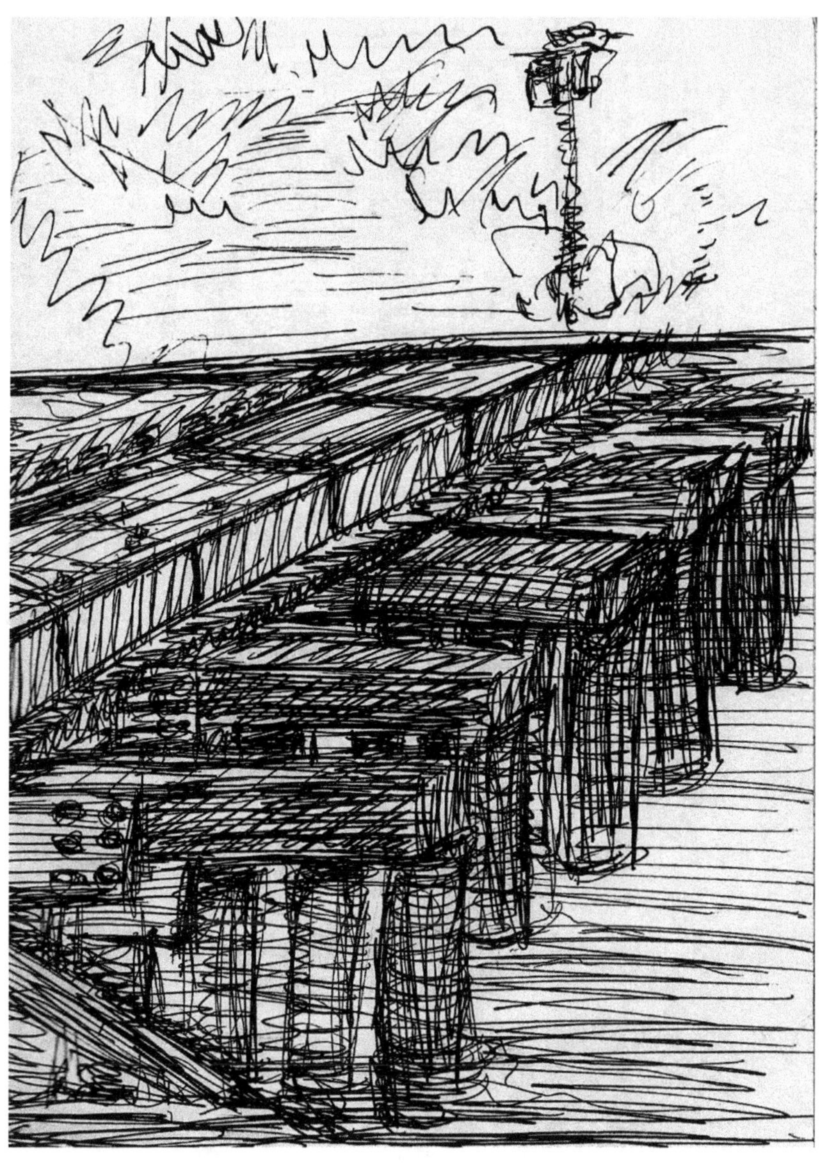

She knew where she wanted to walk.

Elevation, not destination.

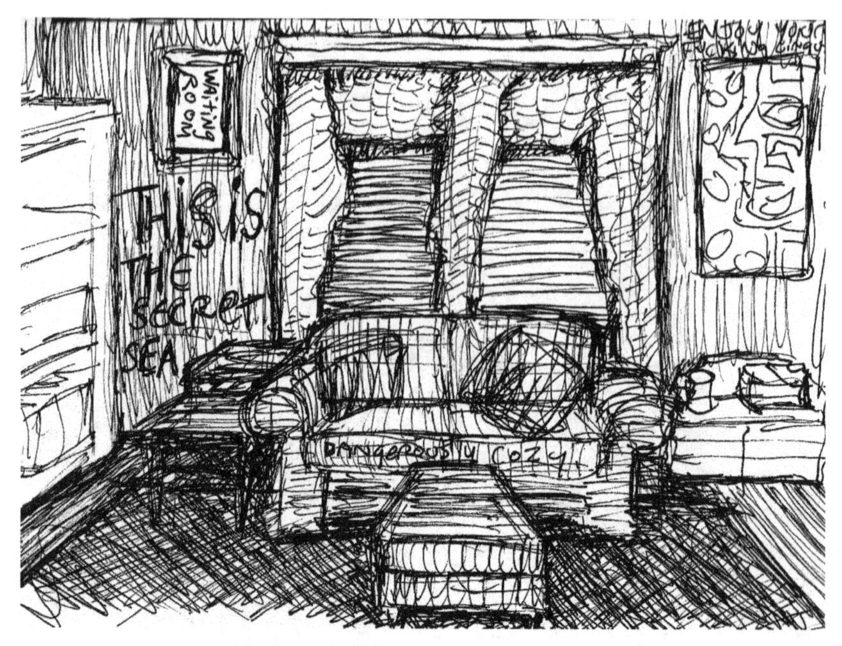


What oceans we curtain away.

How we let ourselves slip

when no eyes are upon us.

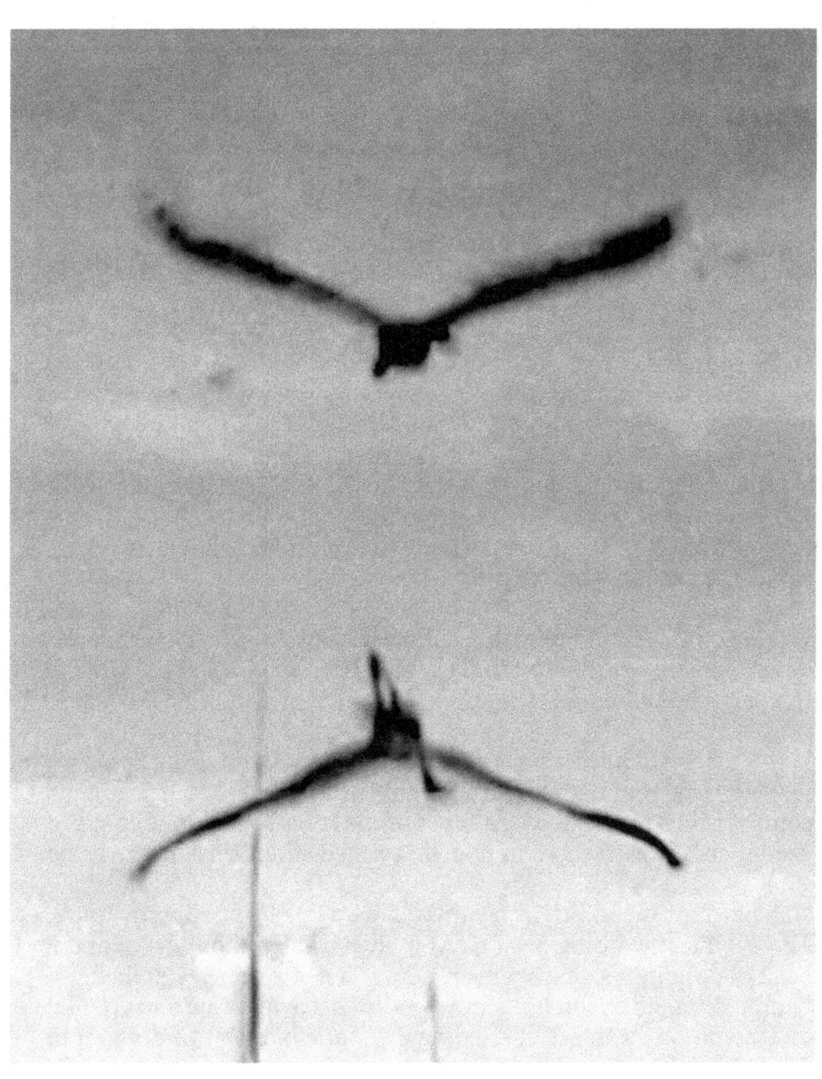

## Odds & Ends At The End

All of the sketches in Finding The Secret Sea were done by Eric C. Harrison. They were started in November, 2011 and were completed in February, 2012. Harrison sketches, nearly every day, during his trip to and from work to curb anxiety and paranoia.

Most of the sketches were done with pigment liners or liquid ink pens on 5x8 inch sketch paper. Many were done on moving trains and buses or while waiting at their respective depots and are primarily composed of what was seen in a glance and sketched out in a few minutes. Some of the images more obviously drawn from fantasy were also done in transit, but were drawn to avoid even having to look up from the page in the first place.

Some of the sketches were done in and around his house in Saltmarsh and from points along a nearby river where he walks his dogs. Though he would not tell me which were drawn in what places, some of the out of doors sketches were done in various locations including Salem, Beverly, Lynn, Rockport and Gloucester.

Fans of Harrison's music may recognize members of his current project, B9K9, in what he calls "sketch cameos."

When he presented me with a gallows copy of Finding The Secret Sea, Harrison had the original sketches in hand and said "Most of the pages are about 10 to 25 minutes worth of sketching."

It was also explained that some of the images in the test copies needed to be redone, so he'd brought the original sketches along for comparison's sake. I noticed most of these had been done in pen, not much pre-sketched in pencil. I asked about this and he told me,

"It's hard for me to put into words ... why I use pen, directly to paper. There's like...no going back ... you have what you put down and it has to be right, because you can't erase it. Sometimes you have to bend the image. Sketching and doodling is a very raw and true form of illustration as an art. I'm being dramatic but it's like doing it in ink is like when you chisel a rock - you have one chance. Doing it on bumpy bus rides was... is, probably a pointless challenge ... and well, annoying. But it keeps me busy and preoccupies me. Keeps my head quiet. Or it does the opposite ..."

I was told also that "… there was no intention of anything coming of the sketches as a collection." When he ran out of paper Harrison looked through his sketch-book, from cover to cover and felt the suggestion of more than one story coming from the moments captured along his daily rut. He attributes this to the repetition in style of sketching, image type and location.

Harrison, appreciative of Mike Maguire's minimalist style of writing, contacted Maguire by messenger seagull, asking him to write a story that was hidden in a series of freehand sketches he'd done, and the project began.

The text created by Mike Maguire was done in stages from June 2012 to September 2012. Harrison emailed Maguire scans of the sketches about twice a week, sending three or four at a time. Maguire responded to each group of images with text for each picture.

When asked about his part in the project (via electronic communications rather than messenger seagull). Maguire's first response was that it made his summer better.

He went on to tell me, "The images would bring out whatever I had been turning over in my head and the bits of writing I did about them always helped me think things through. Doing things like this is the cheapest way I know of gaining clarity."

"It was always done in a very relaxed way. Just bits at a time now and then and never a deadline. There was no pressure to affect my writing with anything that was not a genuine reaction to the sketches. Instead of feeling like the writing of a book, it felt only like being the subject of a very strange Rorschach Test."

Eric C. Harrison did the cover art with scratchboard in September, 2012 when the project's first draft was completed. The two photos of the great blue heron and the picture of the cormorants were taken by Harrison in September, 2012.

- S. Spectre,<br>MPP, Editor.

October 5, 2012

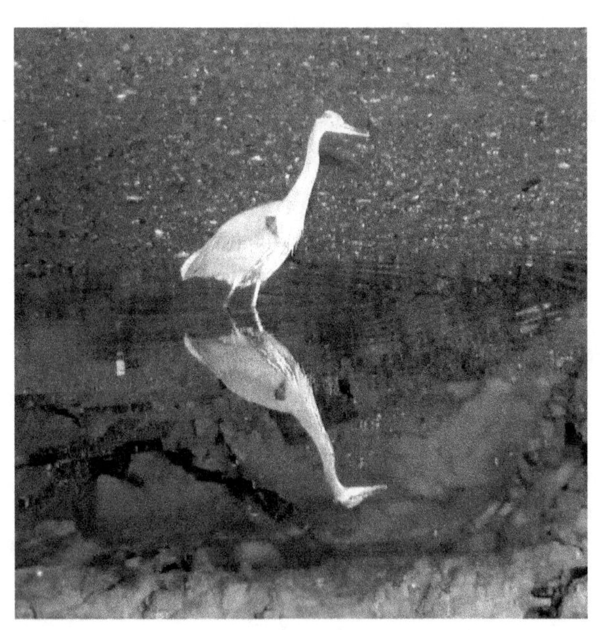

www.ingramcontent.com/pod-product-compliance
Lightning Source LLC
LaVergne TN
LVHW010940110826
845149LV00013B/2696
* 9 7 8 0 9 8 8 8 0 4 0 3 6 *